SU

Cherry Mills takes the job as Senior Staff Nurse on
the Gynae ward at St Monica's so that she can be
near Scott Nicholson. But what chance has her love
for the handsome consultant when it seems that both
Sister Vinton and her cousin Margot have prior
claims on him?

X

SURGEON'S CHOICE

BY

HAZEL FISHER

MILLS & BOON LIMITED
London · Sydney · Toronto

First published in Great Britain 1984
by Mills & Boon Limited, 15–16 Brook's Mews,
London W1A 1DR

ISBN 0 263 74598 8

Set in 10 on 12pt Linotron Times
03–0384–54,265

Photoset by Rowland Phototypesetting Ltd
Bury St Edmunds, Suffolk
Made and printed in Great Britain by
Richard Clay (The Chaucer Press) Ltd
Bungay, Suffolk

CHAPTER ONE

CHERRY Mills's guide, a pretty redhead, chattered on but Cherry heard no more than the occasional word.

So this was St Monica's, where she was to be Senior Staff Nurse on the gynae ward. She gazed up at the tall, grey building, a fairly modern one compared with the London teaching hospital where she had trained.

They were at the rear of the building now, near the staff social club. Jilly Smith, the red-haired nurse, pointed, and Cherry's big brown eyes followed the gesture.

'Yes, a swimming-pool, no less!' Jilly laughed. 'Of course we have to share it with the medical staff, but apart from the housemen we don't get a lot of doctors. Can't see any consultants stripping down to their woolly underwear and diving in!'

Cherry gave her quiet smile and agreed that it was unlikely. Yet she knew of one consultant who might use the pool. Scott Nicholson enjoyed swimming—sports of most kinds. She bit her lip to prevent herself from asking about him.

Scott's light blue, heavy-lidded eyes hovered before her for a second, and Cherry closed her own eyes in anguish. *Forget the man,* her brain advised. *But she loves him,* her heart said wistfully.

'Are you all right?'

5

Cherry opened her eyes to find Jilly peering anxiously at her.

She nodded. 'Mm. I'm fine. Just a bit tired. What's next?' With an effort she forced enthusiasm into her voice, and Jilly seemed satisfied.

The tour was almost over, anyway. The SNO, Personnel, had delegated Jilly to show Cherry around and she'd performed her task efficiently, so much so that Cherry felt she knew the hospital already, and did not feel awkward and gauche as one inevitably did on going to a new job.

At twenty-four Cherry was well experienced, having spent some months as a surgical ward staff nurse before deciding to specialise in gynaecology. Now she wanted about a year at St Monica's before seeking her first sister's post. Her reasons for choosing St Monica's, in the very heart of Kent, were diverse. It was said to have an excellent gynae and obstetric department. She needed a change from the big London hospital. And, most importantly, the consultant gynaecologist was Mr Scott Nicholson, whom Cherry had known in London, when he was Senior Registrar and she a lowly newly-qualified staff nurse.

They became friends, good friends. Cherry found herself falling in love with the tall, athletically-built Scott, and wanted nothing more than to spend the rest of her life taking care of him—soothing his brow when the burdens of his profession proved too much, running her fingers through his crisp black hair, teasing him and making him laugh as she'd done so often before.

Scott, it seemed, did not return her feelings, and though their relationship was intense at first he gradually cooled, mentally planting a barrier between the two of them.

She had never stopped loving him, still kept his photograph by her bed, still kissed it sometimes, feeling foolish as she did so.

When the opportunity arose to work on gynae at St Monica's, where Scott had transferred some months before, Cherry leapt at it.

After Jilly left her, she slowly made her way back to the part of the Nurses' Home set aside for trained staff, wondering yet again if she'd made the right decision. Wondering, too, if Scott would be angry, believing she was deliberately pursuing him.

The next morning, her first on Turner ward, Cherry was near to tears. She'd spent a horribly restless night arguing with herself, wondering if she should have stayed in London. *Was* she pursuing Scott?

If she was honest with herself she knew the answer must be yes, she was. Perhaps he would not see it that way, however, he might have half-forgotten the staff nurse he knew so well.

At Christmas they had exchanged no more than a card, amusing ones depicting cheeky robins. Strange they should choose similar cards. But then they were alike in so many ways, she conceded, her steps faltering as she came within sight of the gynaecological department. They both enjoyed the quieter pleasures of life, took delight in watching a rainbow, a beautiful sunset, admiring the industry of an unusual pearl-grey spider Scott had once found in his parents' garden.

Perhaps they were too much alike. Experts said

opposites attract, so Scott really needed an extrovert personality. Someone like her new ward sister, Stella Vinton, who greeted Cherry at the door of Turner ward.

Stella was a bright, bubbly redhead of about thirty, Cherry judged. Plump, with a bustling, no-nonsense personality. 'Good to see you, Staff Nurse,' Sister said, with a warm smile, her hazel eyes missing no item of Cherry's appearance, and she was glad she'd taken extra care this morning.

The uniform of St Monica's was a far cry from the traditional dress worn at her last hospital. Here the uniform for all ranks was a plain white dress with a zip-front and capacious pockets for the hundred and one items nurses found necessary to carry about. Sisters, however, wore a navy tippet, and a frilly cap tied with ribbons under the chin, the sort of cap Cherry had worn as a staff nurse in London. In addition, Sister Vinton wore a starched apron over her dress.

Staff nurses wore plain white paper caps, the butterfly caps in starched linen being reserved for students and pupils, and Cherry was glad she had never been required to wrestle with them.

Now Cherry fought down the urge to tuck away a non-existent stray blonde hair. Her hair was short, neat and gently curved into her neck. Sister's hair was longer and curly, but still clear of her collar.

'I know you saw over the ward yesterday so there's no need to do the guided tour again,' Sister was saying, and Cherry immediately gave the woman her whole attention.

Whatever Scott might think of her arrival at St Monica's, she *was* keen on gynae, keen on learning all she could about her chosen speciality, and if he thought she was chasing him it was just too bad.

Turner ward was set out on modern lines. The long, dreary wards were a thing of the past and now each wardlet had only four beds, all of them branching off from a central corridor, the nurses' station being strategically placed in the centre.

'We're full at the moment. As usual,' Sister said ruefully. 'We never get a moment's peace and the waiting list is as long as your arm! With Mr Nicholson being away things aren't at all easy.'

Cherry caught her breath. Scott was away? It was probably just as well. It would give her time to settle in.

'Mr Nicholson is the consultant gynaecologist,' Sister put in, as if Cherry had asked. 'Nice enough man. In fact, a very nice man,' she went on, 'but he's a stickler for procedure. Woe betide any nurse who cuts corners.'

'That's as it should be, I suppose,' Cherry offered, and Sister Vinton nodded absently.

Cherry wondered if she ought to tell the older woman she knew Mr Nicholson, but thought better of it. It would not be a good start.

She was immediately plunged into the work of a busy gynae ward. Today she was on middle shift which meant she would finish at five. Tomorrow would be the same, then she had an early shift followed by days off, she noted with surprise.

'That's because I don't do the off-duty any more,' Sister commented. 'I certainly wouldn't give a new nurse days off quite so soon. You will just be getting used to the patients and the routine. When you come back after two days you will have to begin again.'

'Who does arrange the duty rota, then?'

Stella Vinton made a face. 'The Number Seven, Miss Hastings. Part of the drive to give ward sisters less paperwork. It's a good idea but it doesn't always work.'

Sister, after grumbling for a few more minutes, bustled out, and Cherry settled herself down to check the notes on Mrs Grange. It had been an extremely busy morning and she'd had time to do no more than read the Kardex and listen to Sister's debriefing on each patient, making such notes as she had time for.

Now, in what was officially her lunch-break, she could read a few of the case-notes. She intended to get a sandwich from the canteen later.

Alison Grange was in her late forties and had recently undergone a total hysterectomy. Because she was nearing the menopause, hysterectomy was considered to be the most suitable treatment. Her pre-operative condition had led to excessively heavy menstrual periods and severe anaemia, after several weeks of no menstrual loss at all.

Cherry saw Scott's firm, bold handwriting on the notes. Because of the patient's predisposition to malignancy, an hysterectomy was advised, but both Mrs Grange and her husband had opposed the idea for some time, seeing it perhaps as the ending of the woman's life-cycle, the beginning of the end. She wondered how Scott had managed to persuade them.

Poor Mrs Grange, whose personality was unable to accept the inevitable. Sister had pointed her out as a moaner, a depressed, labile person, and Cherry was glad to read something of the background. She would try to talk to the patient, let her express her fears.

Though there was little enough time to talk to the ladies, Cherry reflected, closing the notes and picking up her bag preparatory to dashing out for the sandwich.

'Aha! And who might you be?' a pleasant tenor voice enquired, and Cherry smiled uncertainly at the fairly short, thickset man who placed his briefcase on Sister's chair.

'I'm the new staff nurse—Cherry Mills, sir,' she explained, adding the 'sir' since he seemed to be of some importance.

'Hm. And very nice, too. I'm Donald Atkinson, general surgeon.' Mr Atkinson held out a large hand with a smile that was warm and friendly, and she found herself responding to his ready charm.

So much so that they were chatting like old friends when Sister Vinton returned to her office.

Cherry saw Sister's eyes narrow, and hastily she bid them both goodbye before hurrying to the canteen. Evidently Mr Atkinson was a favourite of Sister's and Cherry had no desire to rush in where angels might fear to tread!

Mr Atkinson had come to see a patient and Cherry meant to ask Sister which one and why. She couldn't recall anything relevant on the Kardex but there was a note in the ward diary that he would be calling.

She frowned, and someone sighed at her elbow. She glanced up in surprise, then smiled at the nurse who eased her plump body into the chair opposite.

'Hi. I'm Hedy Graham. Staff Nurse, Maddison ward. That's general surgery,' the blonde newcomer announced, setting out her lunch and placing the tray by the side of the table.

Cherry introduced herself, feeling less alone now. True, she'd got on well with the other staff on Turner, but she could not see any of them in the canteen. She was glad now she had opted for a quick salad rather than simply taking a sandwich out into the grounds to eat. She questioned Hedy about Mr Atkinson.

'I didn't know who he was at first. Then we got talking and it wasn't until Sister came back that I realised how long we'd been chatting,' Cherry explained, and Hedy laughed, big white teeth gleaming.

'He's like that. Lovely personality. But I'd swop him for that surgeon of yours,' Hedy went on, and Cherry's heart skipped a beat.

'You mean Mr Nicholson?' Her voice quivered but the other nurse appeared not to notice.

'That's the one. You met him yet? No, you wouldn't have. He's at some conference,' Hedy continued. 'Boy, is he something! Big blue eyes, full of cold passion.'

Cherry's lips twitched as she tried not to laugh. 'If his eyes are cold they can hardly be full of passion,' she pointed out, but she knew quite well what Hedy meant.

Scott's deep set eyes might appear chilly at first glance, being a pale blue, but one look from those sleepy-looking eyes was enough to send a girl crazy and Cherry was no exception.

Hedy merely laughed. 'He's Sister Vinton's pet though. Be warned,' she finished, as they strolled through the canteen doors together.

Cherry hardly registered Hedy's friendly wave as they moved off in opposite directions. *Scott Nicholson is Sister's pet. Be warned*. The words made her turn cold, all the joy and laughter draining from her.

Sister's hands were bare of rings, she'd noticed. Yet that meant nothing in itself. Even married nurses did not always wear a wedding ring on duty. She must find out. What a laugh it would be if Sister Vinton and Scott were engaged!

The laugh would be on you, Staff Nurse Mills, she acknowledged bitterly, wishing again that she hadn't come to St Monica's.

Sister's manner was distant, less friendly, when Cherry returned to the ward and she wondered if Hedy might be wrong. Could it be that Mr Atkinson was the special one in her life? She fervently hoped so.

'I'm away to lunch now you're back.' Sister's voice was sharp, yet Cherry knew she was a few minutes early rather than late. 'After lunch I'm over at the school of nursing giving a lecture, so you will have to cope.'

Idly Sister flicked the pages of the Kardex. 'We aren't expecting any admissions, so you shouldn't have any problems. Staff Nurse Evans is due back any minute so you can lean on her, if necessary.' Staff Nurse Evans was the junior staff nurse on the ward, a briskly efficient nurse, and Cherry relaxed. Being left in charge of a new ward in a new hospital wasn't the ideal situation.

Yet somehow she coped. As Sister Vinton said, the ward was busy but there were no great problems.

Many of the patients were very short-stay and were in for minor conditions, but there were three post-hysterectomy patients. One of them, a Mrs Bailey, was not expected to survive long after discharge, and Cherry made time to sit by her bed, encouraging her to express her fears, if she could.

Mrs Bailey had not been told of the prognosis, but

Cherry thought the woman suspected the worse. Surgeons did not always give patients credit for much intelligence and she meant to have a word with Scott about it when the opportunity arose.

She'd learned that the consultant was due back on the ward on Wednesday, though he would probably pop in before, and the thought sent a prickle of awareness down her spine.

Cherry shivered slightly, and Mrs Bailey was quick to notice the gesture. Sighing a little, the patient eased herself into a more comfortable position, her gaze quizzical.

'Unhappy thoughts, Staff Nurse?' she queried softly, and Cherry squeezed her hand, trying to instil some of her own young, vigorous life into the woman.

'Can't tell you my thoughts. You might be jealous!' she said lightly, and a flicker of humour appeared in the woman's dull brown eyes. Cherry chatted for a few minutes more, aware that Mrs Bailey wanted to ask about her condition but would not.

Feeling that she'd achieved very little, Cherry returned to the office in time to see the junior student, Nurse MacDonald, taking in a cup of tea. In her other hand she held a plate of biscuits, and Cherry raised a brow enquiringly. As far as she knew, the office was empty.

'Oh, Staff! I'm sorry but he said not to bother you!' the student exclaimed, her face flushed. 'I was going to look for you, honestly, but he said it didn't matter.'

The teacup wobbled in its saucer, and Cherry smiled reassuringly at the worried nurse.

'I'm sure you meant to seek me but *who* said it didn't

matter?' The office door was almost closed and Cherry was annoyed, though not with the nurse. If a doctor was on the ward it was discourteous of him or her not to see the nurse in charge.

Before the little student could answer, a cold voice asked testily if they would be quiet, and Cherry went hot, then cold.

Scott Nicholson's voice!

'It's Mr Nicholson, Staff,' Nurse MacDonald informed her unnecessarily, and Cherry nodded absently.

'Please Staff. What shall I do about his tea? He'll be cross if it's cold.'

'I'll take it to him, Nurse,' Cherry said firmly, taking the crockery from the student's unresisting fingers.

Annoyed at Scott for coming on to the ward unannounced and demanding tea, Cherry marched in.

Scott's dark head was bent over some notes as he sat at Sister Vinton's desk, and he did not immediately glance up.

Cherry stared at his head for a moment, longing sweeping over her. 'Your tea, Mr Nicholson,' she said crisply, drawing forward a blotter on which to place the cup and saucer. '*And* biscuits,' she added, tartly.

That did it. Scott Nicholson's head shot up in surprise. His pale eyes narrowed incredulously, then a slow smile spread across his lean, handsome face.

'Cherry! Cherry Mills! What on earth . . . ?' He rose slowly, surveying Cherry, who felt like a gawky teen-ager. Why, she was even blushing!

The more she tried to control her rising colour, the worse it became, and Scott's smile became a chuckle.

Wishing she could sink through the floor, Cherry

laced her fingers together and gazed at a point above his head. She could think of nothing to say, nothing at all. How stupid he must think her!

'Well, well. Cherry.' Scott sat down again, motioning her to do the same.

Cherry perched on the edge of the hard chair opposite the desk, her face still hot.

Scott, still smiling, was surveying her keenly, and Cherry urged him to drink his tea before it got cold.

'Ah, yes. Tea and biscuits. How very kind of you,' he murmured, and Cherry bit back a sharp retort.

'Go on. Tear me off a strip,' he invited, stirring his tea, and Cherry smiled, aware that he had read her mind.

'I was thinking you have a nerve coming on to a ward unannounced, demanding tea, *and* ignoring the nurse in charge,' she said cheekily, adding 'sir' as an after-thought.

Scott gave her his lazy grin. 'You are quite right, Staff Nurse. Or is it Sister? No, there wouldn't be two of you.'

'Still Staff Nurse,' she admitted, trying not to stare at his dear, lean face. It was a losing battle. And he knew it. Knew the effect one glance from those sensuous eyes would have on her.

He gave her the full treatment, leaning back in Sister's chair, arms folded behind his head, still smiling, his eyes hooded now, concealing his thoughts.

He must think I'm here because of him, Cherry reflected, unhappily aware of how it must look to him. Well, she would not fall into his arms. Nor would she embarrass him. She would play it cool and see what the future held.

It was again as if he'd read her mind. 'What brings you

to St Monica's, Staff Nurse Mills?' he drawled, and Cherry swallowed, nervously.

'A change of scenery,' she said brightly. 'St Monica's has an excellent gynae department,' she hurried on, and was amazed to see a flicker of disappointment cross the surgeon's face. Surely he did not expect her to admit she had come because of him?

'What brought *you* to St Monica's?' she countered, and he shrugged, before drinking thirstily.

'Aren't you having a cup?' he queried, then ate two chocolate biscuits after she'd refused. 'Needed a change of scenery, too,' he said at last, his face solemn now.

He steepled his long, clever fingers, staring into space. 'Our old hospital—I found it . . . confining,' he went on. 'I needed freedom to develop my career. No ties here.'

He gave her a sharp glance, and Cherry nodded dully. That was meant as a warning. Do not pursue me. I want my freedom. No ties. He couldn't have made it much plainer.

Swallowing her disappointment she rose, collecting the empty cup. 'I'll leave you to your notes, Mr Nicholson,' she murmured and was at the door before he called out,

'It *is* good to see you again, Cherry. We must have a night out in merry old Tunbridge Wells—for old times' sake,' he added, and Cherry nodded her acceptance, anxious to leave.

For old times' sake. In memory of a good friendship, now dead. Was that all the future held for her and Scott?

Wednesday was Scott's round-day and Sister was already on the ward when Cherry arrived at seven-thirty. Scott had still been on the ward when Sister returned from her lecture on the Monday, and the two of them had been closeted in the office for an hour, with the door closed.

Hedy Graham was right, then. Scott Nicholson *was* a favourite of Sister's.

Cherry shrugged aside all personal thoughts. What mattered was getting the patients and their notes ready for the consultant's round.

Sister glanced up as Cherry bade her a quiet 'good morning'. Her glance was frosty and Cherry wondered what she had done.

She didn't have long to wonder. Once she'd heard the report and dismissed the night nurses, Sister allotted various tasks to each of her staff and got Cherry to mark the ward duty book up accordingly.

When the others trooped out, intent on setting the ward to rights, Cherry moved to follow them but Sister Vinton called her back. 'Not you, Staff Nurse. We have one or two matters to iron out.'

Cherry turned, her gaze wary. She could not recall omitting to do anything in connection with the ward work, so the bone of contention could only be Scott Nicholson.

Sister need not worry. What had happened between Cherry and Scott was in the past now. If Scott's future belonged to Sister Vinton, so be it.

She sat down as directed, and waited.

CHAPTER TWO

SISTER gave her a sharp glance. 'I know you have come from the big city, Nurse. I realise that standards in London are . . . different,' she said slowly, and Cherry frowned at this veiled criticism of her old hospital.

'Here at St Monica's we do expect senior staff to maintain a very high standard,' she went on. 'You're a senior person in our hierarchy, even if you might not think so. When I came back on Monday you were being most familiar with Mr Atkinson. Then, later, there was Mr Nicholson,' Sister continued, warming to her theme, and Cherry reddened.

'I'm sure you meant nothing improper, Staff Nurse, but there *is* a certain barrier between consultants and ourselves and we must try to maintain it.'

'Yes, of course, Sister. I'm sorry, Sister,' Cherry answered automatically, knowing from past experience that it was always better to apologise to ward sisters even when she wasn't in the wrong.

Sister visibly relaxed, having made her point, and a chastened Cherry slipped out of the office and went about her tasks, hoping she had heard the end of the matter. The slur on her former hospital was one she could not forgive. It set far higher standards of behaviour, both on and off-duty than St Monica's, but she could not expect Sister Vinton to understand that.

19

Mr Nicholson was a few minutes late for his round, and Sister spent the time fussing, adjusting a coverlet here, a bed wheel there.

Cherry saw the patients trying to hide their amusement, one of them whispering to a newer patient that Sister was always like this on round-days. It was a stage whisper which carried clearly to Cherry and to Sister herself.

When Scott finally arrived he gave no indication that he knew Cherry, to her relief. Beyond a cursory 'Good morning, Staff Nurse,' he ignored her, concentrating all his considerable charm on Sister Vinton, who beamed throughout the round.

Cherry, who wasn't required for the round, settled herself in the office and selected a few notes to read. SEN Peters was at the nurses' station and could ring through to the office if necessary.

They had twenty-eight patients and as Sister had said, there was a considerable waiting list. Scott Nicholson took gynae Outpatients on Friday and Cherry supposed there would be a few more names to add to the list after his clinic.

A never-ending stream. Then there was the obstetric side. Scott was extremely busy and Cherry felt for him. Being a nurse was hard enough, particularly if one was trained, with all the responsibilities that brought, but for the senior doctor or surgeon, the responsibilities were enormous. Even house doctors carried a great burden but they could always ask the opinion of registrar or consultant. For men like Scott Nicholson the buck stopped there.

Cherry's brown eyes were thoughtful as she left the

sanctuary of the office and went to speak to some of the patients Scott and his entourage had already seen.

Mrs Bailey was one of these, her bed being nearest the office, and Cherry knew Scott had seen the woman first. 'What did Mr Nicholson say?' she asked gently, patting Mrs Bailey's hand.

The grey-faced, grey-haired woman reached for her box of tissues and Cherry assisted her, then smoothed the bedclothes and adjusted the pillows. They were automatic gestures. Making the patients comfortable became second nature after a time.

Mrs Bailey dabbed at her eyes, then shrugged. It was a weary, defeated gesture, and Cherry's smile slipped a little. Had she been told? she wondered, but thought it unlikely. Sister would have mentioned it to all the ward staff so that they could cope with the new situation.

'What do they ever say?' Mrs Bailey whispered, her eyes not meeting Cherry's. 'Everything yet nothing. He's nice, though. He's got kind eyes and warm hands.'

Cherry laughed softly. 'That's very important. I think some doctors put their hands in the icebox before they examine patients!'

She was rewarded by the faintest of smiles. The entourage was by now nearly at the last bed, and Cherry slipped her hand out of Mrs Bailey's with a whispered, 'I'll see you later'.

It wasn't the thought that Sister would be annoyed with her for not being in the office when the surgeon finished, it was the sound of quiet weeping that drew Cherry away.

It was Shirley Easton again. Her problem was only a

comparatively minor one and she'd had a biopsy, no
more. Nothing to be weeping about, Cherry thought,
annoyed because it was Mrs Bailey who needed the extra
attention.

Catching the eye of the second-year pupil nurse, who
was doing the chores, Cherry whispered that she should
stay within easy reach of Mrs Bailey.

Then she crossed purposefully to the section where
Shirley Easton lay. As soon as the round was over the
patients would be up and about again and Cherry intended making sure that Shirley had something with
which to occupy herself. She . . .

'Staff!' Sister Vinton's voice was sharp and brooked
no argument, and Cherry had to make do with a warm
smile for the very young Shirley before hurrying to the
office.

Mr Nicholson had halted in the doorway, frowning a
little as his eyes followed Cherry's steady progress.
Feeling his eyes upon her, her steps faltered. She didn't
want to fall foul of Sister just yet and it wouldn't do if she
saw the interest the consultant was taking.

When Cherry arrived at the office, Sister was behind
the desk, with Scott Nicholson now in an easy chair by
her side, his notes propped up against a corner of the
desk. His registrar and the female house surgeon had
also been found chairs but there was none for Cherry,
who stood just inside the door, and waited to hear the
consultant's conclusions.

Then, to her horror, Scott stood and offered her his
chair. Face aflame, and aware of Sister's incredulous
gaze, Cherry took the proffered seat, knowing that a
refusal would anger him. Scott Nicholson had a biting

tongue when he chose to use it and their former friendship would not help her.

Pleasing him meant annoying Sister Vinton and Cherry wasn't sure which was the greater evil.

The debriefing proceeded, Cherry very conscious of Scott's nearness, for he lounged against the wall beside her. If she put out a hand she could have touched his long, lean thigh.

On the other side of Cherry, Sister sat very erect and silently drumming her fingers on the desk top. She had to contain her ire until the doctors had left but Cherry knew that it would spill over afterwards.

'Tell me about Mrs Bailey,' Scott asked suddenly, and Sister gave him a rundown on both her physical and mental state.

Cherry was surprised and pleased that Sister had noticed the patient's mental state at all. When she had finished, Cherry added her comments, whether Scott wanted them or not.

She pointed out that the patient suspected the worst but that no one had told her anything, though the husband knew the poor prognosis. 'She cries a lot, sir,' she went on, aware that she had his whole attention. 'She's worried sick yet doesn't want to voice her fears.'

'Naturally, Nurse,' Sister cut in. 'She *doesn't* want to speak about her fears. That's the crucial point. She doesn't *want* to know.'

'I think she does . . .' Cherry began, then subsided. It wasn't her place to argue with Sister in front of the consultant.

'What does Mr Bailey say? You've seen him?' Scott turned to his registrar.

Eventually it was decided that Sister would see the man and ask his opinion of the desirability of telling his wife, something no one else appeared to have done.

Pleased, Cherry sat back, then Scott's voice spoke, almost to her alone. 'Remember, Staff Nurse, there are such things as miracles. In surgery we have all experienced them. Take away a person's hope, and what remains?'

Contrite, Cherry glanced up at him. Blue eyes smiled into her own and she felt as if *she* had experienced a miracle. The sun shone for her alone. His lazy smile had that effect on people, staff as well as patients.

'Yes, remember that, Staff Nurse,' Sister said grimly, before flipping the Kardex to the next patient's name.

Aware that she was living on borrowed time where Sister was concerned, Cherry took no further part in the conversation, contenting herself with making copious notes. She would discuss these with the other nurses at a more convenient time.

'We ought to be off soon,' Scott said as the junior brought in a tray of coffee, and Sister turned to Cherry.

'As Mr Nicholson has finished, perhaps you would stay at the station, Staff Nurse. Relieve Nurse Peters.'

Dismissed, and with the tantalising aroma of strong coffee in her nostrils, Cherry quietly left, and was sitting at the nurses' station when the junior nurse brought her a cup brimming with coffee. So full that there was a pool of coffee in the saucer.

'That's kind of you, Nurse.' Cherry was surprised that Sister had thought about her.

'It was Mr Nicholson's idea, Staff,' Nurse MacDonald

assured her, before scurrying away, leaving a disquieted Cherry to drink the scalding liquid.

Mr Nicholson's idea. She might have known. He was such a kind man but what would his kindness cost her?

Soon it was time for her lunch but still she stayed in the main ward, keeping a careful eye on the patients. Now and then she glanced towards the office, half-inclined to go and tell Sister she was going to lunch. But that would mean leaving the patients, for there were no other nurses within calling distance.

The patients had all gone back to bed ready for their own lunches and Cherry saw the trolley arrive.

Knowing she wasn't to be relieved, she hurried up the ward just as the office door opened and Sister appeared, all smiles.

'Not gone to lunch, Staff?' She sounded surprised, which was nonsense, but Cherry let it pass. 'I'll serve, Staff Nurse. You run along,' Sister instructed, and Cherry was glad to leave.

Sister was pleasant for the rest of the day, Cherry's shift finishing at four, while Sister was due to stay until five.

Cherry soon found out why. Sister wanted a favour. 'I'm out to dance the night away next Thursday, Staff,' she announced, as soon as the patients' teas were finished. 'I wonder—could you do me a favour and work for me that evening? I'll sort it out with Miss Hastings.'

Cherry was happy to oblige. Her own social life was almost non-existent these days, though she'd promised to take in a film with Jilly Smith some time, but no date had been fixed.

'Glad to help, Sister. Going somewhere nice?' Cherry asked, as she thumbed through the filing cabinet.

'Mm. The Majestic, no less!' Sister laughed, and Cherry wondered who was taking her. She really must find out if Sister was married.

'You didn't tell me you knew Scott Nicholson before,' Sister went on reproachfully, and Cherry went cold.

'Didn't I?' she parried. 'I . . . I thought it better not to mention it,' she went on lightly, turning towards her senior.

Their eyes met, and Sister nodded as if satisfied. 'Yes, probably as well. People would put two and two together. Especially as you came from the same hospital.'

'That's what I thought, Sister. I wouldn't want anyone to think that Scott . . . That Mr Nicholson and myself were in any way . . .' Cherry halted, but Sister seemed to understand.

'People *will* say that, Nurse. The hospital grapevine likes nothing better than that sort of tasty titbit to feed on. Like fertilizer to a plant, that sort of gossip,' Sister carried on, but she didn't seem unduly perturbed and Cherry relaxed, pleased the woman wasn't going to make an issue of it.

'Just as long as you keep a polite barrier between Mr Nicholson and yourself, there might not be much harm done.'

'Yes of course, Sister,' Cherry murmured. 'Did Mr Nicholson mention that I knew him? I suppose he must have done. No one else here knows.'

'He mentioned it in passing,' Sister affirmed. 'Seemed astonished you hadn't told *me*.'

Cherry shifted uncomfortably, but Sister did not apparently expect a comment, for she went on, 'It doesn't matter. Everyone here knows that Sco . . . Mr Nicholson and I are . . . friends.'

Cherry bit back her gasp of surprise, but Sister Vinton's eyes narrowed as she smiled at her.

'I hope—in the not too distant future—that Mr Nicholson and I will have an announcement to make. But that is for your ears alone, Staff Nurse,' Sister warned, and Cherry murmured that she would keep the secret.

When four o'clock came Cherry could have cried with relief. She wanted only to escape to the sanctuary of her room and have a good cry, but even that was denied her for Jilly Smith was waiting for her at the ward door.

'That film's on next week, Cherry,' she enthused, and if Cherry's smile was weary Jilly appeared not to notice. 'Shall we say Thursday?'

'What? Oh, yes. No! Sister's out that evening. I'm covering for her. What about Wednesday?' Cherry said without enthusiasm. Sister and Scott Nicholson. If only she'd known! What a blind fool she'd been.

Fool to think she could revive what had been, breathe life into cold ashes.

'Wednesday then,' Jilly was saying. 'Want to come to my room?' By this time they had walked to the entrance of the Nurses' Home, Cherry saw with surprise. She hadn't been aware of walking at all.

'I'll soon have the kettle boiling,' Jilly went on. 'You look jaded.'

Cherry *felt* jaded but company was the last thing she wanted. She began to shake her head then her eyes widened with shock as the tall, dark man rose from his seat in the entrance hall.

Jilly glanced from the consultant to Cherry, then back again. From her expression it wasn't difficult to read her mind and Cherry almost groaned aloud. Instead, she went forward politely to greet Scott Nicholson, and introduced Jilly, who had never worked on his wards.

Jilly's green eyes were almost round in amazement as she breezed away and Cherry hoped she wasn't a gossip. If Sister found out that Scott was visiting Staff Nurse Mills in the Nurses' Home she would be less than pleased.

'Thought we might fix up that meal I was talking about,' Scott said affably, his smile sending desire coursing along Cherry's veins, and she put out a hand as if to ward him off, then dropped it to her side, feeling foolish.

'Yes. Oh, I'm not sure . . .' she began but Scott was already making for the stairs.

'This way, is it?' he queried, one foot on the first stair, and Cherry gaped.

'Your room, Cherry. Will you lead the way?' he went on, still smiling, and Cherry found her voice.

'I can't take you up there!' she squeaked.

'Why on earth not? This is the trained staff section,' he pointed out, reasonably. 'Even I had a flatlet here when I first arrived. Not getting prudish are you?' he chuckled, his eyes warm, and Cherry felt herself colour.

'We can talk downstairs, Scott. There's a perfectly good lounge,' she said, but he waved the idea way.

'I know there is a lounge. It's occupied. Come on, Cherry. I won't eat you!'

She smiled weakly and went on ahead of him. She

could feel his warm breath on her neck and she quickened her pace, wanting to get a date fixed and him out of the Nurses' Home as soon as possible.

She waved a hand in welcome after she unlocked her door. 'This is it. Staff Nurse's bed-sitter!' she announced, brightly, and he followed her, closing the door behind him.

It was a big room, for which she was thankful. Being sparsely furnished there was little choice over seating, and Scott settled himself in the only armchair while Cherry sat gingerly on the very edge of the bed, feeling acutely uncomfortable that she had to entertain him in a bedroom.

She was glad that the photograph of Scott she kept by her bed was tucked away out of sight. It came out only at night.

He crossed his legs and gazed around with evident satisfaction. 'Nice big room. Do much entertaining, do you?'

'What? Oh, no. Not much. I've only just arrived, after all.'

There was a small silence and Cherry racked her brains to find a safe topic for conversation.

'You could do with a few ornaments. Did you bring any from your last place?' he asked, and Cherry was glad of the innocuous topic.

'Only a vase. My ward sister gave it to me when I left.' Glad to move, Cherry shot up and retrieved the brown glazed vase from the bottom of the wardrobe.

'Hm. Pretty. She must have thought a lot of you, Cherry.'

'I hope so. We certainly got on well.' Much better than

I will with Sister Vinton, she added silently, and Scott chuckled as if he knew about the difficult situation on the ward.

Loath though she was to mention the woman, Cherry thought it best to bring the matter into the open. 'I didn't realise you and Sister Vinton were friends,' she said quietly, and waited for his reaction, every nerve jangling. If only he would deny it!

'Didn't you?' He sounded bored. 'Thought the whole of St Monica's knew. Keeps the grapevine happy.'

'Yes, of course,' she murmured unhappily, wondering how she might extricate herself from the embarrassing situation.

'Diana was asking after you. She wondered if I ever saw you now.'

Diana was Scott's married sister. 'I like Diana. And that cute little boy!' Cherry's eyes lit up with remembrance. Diana's son, Nigel, was a poppet and Cherry would have liked a son just like him. Her son and Scott's.

Her face clouded, and she picked up the vase and put it back in the wardrobe, glad of some activity, however pointless.

'Remember when we took Nigel to the fair? Last summer, wasn't it?' Scott leaned back in the armchair as he spoke, surveying her through half-closed lids, and Cherry nodded.

'You won a doll for me and a goldfish for him.' She didn't tell Scott she still had the rag doll with its gaudily painted face and cheap nylon outfit.

'He's still got that fish. It was pretty. Black and gold with long fins, as I recall,' Scott went on, his eyes completely closed now.

Pleased because she could feast her eyes on his dear face without him being aware of it, Cherry laughed. 'It *was* black and gold. I suppose it's grown now? And changed colour?'

'Mm. Completely gold now. And much bigger—not so elegant. Looks more like a sardine! Enough to put me off eating sardines, I can tell you!'

'I didn't think consultants *did* eat sardines,' Cherry laughed. 'Surely you've joined the smoked salmon and caviar set now?'

'No, not quite, but I'm working on it,' Scott admitted, his eyes still tightly closed, and Cherry admired the long sweep of his dark lashes against his tanned face.

It had been a long hot summer with plenty of sunshine, and Scott obviously hadn't wasted any of it. Did Sister Vinton join him in his sunbathing sessions?

The idea was disquieting, and she closed her mind, content just to sit and stare at the face of the man she loved. If only she could turn back the clock.

'Where shall we dine?' he asked suddenly, opening his eyes and catching her staring.

Embarrassed, she gave a half-laugh. 'Anywhere. Anywhere you like. I'm not familiar with the area, Scott.'

'I'll fix something up. Shall we say a fortnight Saturday? Can you get the weekend off?'

She frowned, unsure of her duties. Unsure, too, about accepting the invitation. 'Do you think we should? Go out together, I mean?' she floundered. 'Sister might not like it.'

'She doesn't own me, Cherry,' he said sharply. 'It's only for old times' sake. Celebrating a friendship that once was,' he was quick to point out, and Cherry pinned a smile to her pretty mouth, unwilling to let him see the tears so near the surface.

'Fine. I'll try to wangle the Saturday evening off. I'll let you know definitely,' she assured him, standing up, relieved that he would be going.

'Come to think of it, Stella usually has weekends,' he murmured, settling back in the chair, apparently not at all anxious to leave.

It allowed Cherry a way out of the invitation. 'In that case I can't come. Not on a Saturday then. I couldn't ask Sister to exchange duties with me,' she said firmly.

'Why ever not? She wouldn't hesitate.' Scott sounded affronted, as if he knew she was trying to wriggle off the hook, and she lost her temper.

'I've already said it isn't such a good idea, Scott! It doesn't affect you but she *is* my ward sister and it could poison our professional relationship,' she flared, hating herself for losing control. Really, he was being thick today! It was all his fault.

'My dear girl, you're seeing difficulties where none exist! Stella hasn't a jealous bone in her body. I'll mention to her that I'm taking you out,' he went on, smiling slightly, and Cherry could have hit him.

In fact, she took a step towards him in her fury, then stopped, letting him see the anguish in her eyes instead.

'Please, Scott, no! I . . . I'll come out with you. Just once, for old times' sake, as you said, but Sister mustn't know.'

His expression was inscrutable, then he smiled, displaying even white teeth. He had a beautiful mouth, with a full, sensuous lower lip. A mouth she loved to kiss, and longing swept over her.

Averting her gaze, she smiled at the wall behind him. 'It's getting late. I have to wash my hair before supper.'

Taking the hint he got up, still smiling, his pale eyes mocking her, and she felt gauche, provincial, no longer the sophisticated young woman he had once known.

'Supper isn't yet awhile, Cherry,' he pointed out, towering above her, despite her height, too close for her peace of mind.

'N . . . no, but I've had a hard day. A particularly hard day,' she added, unable to keep the bitterness from her voice.

He shrugged. 'So have I,' he countered, and she immediately felt selfish. If she had problems, his were much greater.

Without thinking, she put her small hand on his sleeve. The cloth was crisp and expensive to the touch, and Cherry snatched her hand away as she realised what she was doing.

Scott made no move towards her, nor did he retreat, and Cherry was confused, wondering anew just what he felt for her these days.

'On early tomorrow?' His voice was gentle, his eyes concerned as he gazed down at her, and she shook her head, moving away.

She did not want his concern, only his love. Or, if she was to be denied that, she would like his friendship. 'No. I'm off tomorrow. And the day after. Sister was moaning about it—just getting me eased into the routine then losing me for two days,' she explained.

'Sister's loss is my gain. Have lunch with me tomorrow,' he invited, and Cherry eyed him, warily.

'No, I won't tell Stella!' he laughed. 'There's an excellent seafood restaurant here. It's a working day for me but I can lunch at one.'

His tone brooked no argument, and Cherry didn't want to refuse, anyway. They arranged to meet outside the restaurant. Scott would drive her back to the hospital afterwards.

Then, arrangements completed, he moved towards the door and Cherry hurried to open it for him. The room would seem lonely once he'd gone. Perversely, she wanted now to prolong his visit, even knowing the dangers.

'See you tomorrow, Cherry. Bye.' After an almost imperceptible hesitation, he leaned forward and pressed his cool lips to her brow. Then he was gone, and Cherry watched his tall, lean figure until it was out of sight round the bend of the twisting stairway.

He'd kissed her! Wonderingly, she pressed a hand to her burning cheek. Then traced the outline of his mouth on her brow.

True, the kiss had been cool, impersonal, much like a kiss exchanged by two women taking leave of each other. Certainly there was nothing sexual about it. It was just a meaningless kiss, she scolded herself. Don't read into it more than he intended.

Nevertheless, she found herself looking forward to the following day's lunch with an eager expectancy she hadn't felt for a very long time.

*

Cherry took extra pains with her appearance the following day, discarding outfit after outfit before settling on the deep blue Scott liked so much.

He preferred her in blue and the cool cotton dress she'd chosen was an old-stager in her wardrobe. Sleeveless, with a round neckline and touches of white broderie anglaise, it suited her cool blonde features and slender figure.

She almost discarded it when she remembered that she'd worn it so often before in London, when Scott had been escorting her. Would he think she'd worn it deliberately?

Shrugging, she decided to take the risk. Men never took that much interest, anyway. If he recalled the dress at all he might think she wore it because she couldn't afford a new one!

She left her face unmade-up except for a trace of pink lipstick. Scott definitely did not like over-painted women. After splashing herself liberally with toilet water rather than using the precious French perfume which had been a gift from Scott in happier days, she was ready.

The sun shone, the traffic was light, and the bus made good time. She hummed a little tune to herself as she walked carefully along in her high-heeled sandals. Knowing he would give her a lift back she'd left her elderly Escort car at the hospital.

She was lunching with Scott. Even if it was only for friendship's sake she didn't care. She would make the most of it, savour every moment. For she recognised that this might be the last time they met socially.

If Sister Vinton had spoken the truth there could well

be an engagement in the offing. No matter how much Scott played down the relationship, Sister seemed very sure it was a serious one.

The sun went momentarily behind a cloud, and Cherry shivered slightly as she reached the restaurant.

CHAPTER THREE

SCOTT had not yet arrived and Cherry waited in the doorway for a few minutes, then began to pace up and down, by which time it was ten past one.

Just as she began to wonder if he had forgotten he arrived, immaculate in a dark grey suit and white shirt, not looking at all hot and bothered even though the temperature was well into the seventies. He did not appear to have hurried.

He frowned when he saw her. 'Surely you went inside? I phoned and asked them to hang on to the table. Got a bit held up,' he explained, urging her forward impatiently.

Sick at heart, Cherry allowed herself to be shunted into the restaurant. He didn't want to lunch with her. She was being a nuisance and he was a busy man, after all.

There was no time for a pre-lunch drink and Scott probably wouldn't want one as he had appointments in the afternoon. Cherry would have been glad of one, even if it was only to drown her sorrows!

Although the restaurant's speciality was seafood, there were other dishes available, and Scott chose melon followed by steak.

Cherry, not wanting to linger over the menu and make him late, chose fruit juice and the seafood omelette. That would not take long to digest.

She forced a bright smile to her face and asked him about his morning.

After giving her a quizzical look, Scott launched into a minute account of his morning's work. So detailed was the account that Cherry suspected he was doing it deliberately. He knew she didn't know what else to talk about, and work was always a safe topic.

'See anything of cousin Margot these days?' he threw in casually as he began on his steak.

Carefully, Cherry lowered her fork upon which she'd speared a prawn. 'Not a lot. I expect I shall see her when I go up to London again.' She kept her voice neutral.

'Nice bit of steak. Beats hospital food. Ah, thank you.' This last remark was to the waiter who refilled the water jug. 'I'm a regular here,' he explained to Cherry, who sipped her drink and nodded.

Was Sister Vinton also a regular? she wondered, taking another sip. As she'd suspected, Scott hadn't wanted alcohol but had chosen a sparkling white wine for her, knowing her preference.

'About Margot,' he went on. 'She drops me a postcard from exotic spots every now and again but I haven't seen her since I left London.'

Innocent blue eyes met hers, and she struggled with that demon, jealousy. His expression was far too innocent, his questions too casual.

Cousin Margot was her second cousin. In her thirties, Margot had never married but had never lacked for male company either. She enjoyed playing the field, as she had confided to Cherry once. She did not intend to be bogged down by domestic chores, children, a husband, a mortgage. Not Margot.

In earlier years she had been a courier for a travel operator, jetting to places Cherry had only dreamed of. Now she was a senior executive in the West End office of the same company.

Margot still got to do quite a bit of travelling but Cherry hadn't known she sent postcards to Scott. It worried her. Not that Margot was exactly predatory, but she was attractive, with long, carelessly waved golden-brown hair and amber eyes. The sort of woman any man would be glad to go home to.

Vivacious, charming, able to take an intelligent interest in any one of a great many subjects, she would be ideal for Scott, Cherry had thought more than once. The attraction of opposites—she herself being far too serious for him.

Scott was eyeing her expectantly, and Cherry dragged her mind back to the present. 'I'll tell her you asked after her,' she said carefully.

'Thanks. She should be due for another big party soon, shouldn't she? Always had at least one a quarter.'

'Yes. I suppose so. She . . . she doesn't . . . I mean, I don't often go to her parties,' Cherry confessed, causing Scott to give her a sharp look.

'That isn't because she doesn't invite you, Cherry. It's because you don't enjoy big, noisy gatherings,' he said quietly, springing to Margot's defence, and Cherry reddened.

'I didn't mean to imply that she never bothered to ask me,' she said, equally quietly. She was near to tears, realising at last why he had invited her out. 'Margot and I haven't a lot in common,' she added, brown eyes sad.

Margot was the nearest she had to a sister, she was her

closest relative. It was unfortunate that there was the age gap, coupled with their totally different outlook on life. To Cherry, life was a serious business. True, she had a sense of humour, but she took her profession seriously, did all she could to improve her knowledge, and privately regarded Margot as frivolous and far too young for her years.

It was a view that might well be coloured by envy, Cherry was honest enough to acknowledge. Women like Margot got more fun out of life than those of a quieter disposition. And Scott had been drawn, briefly, to Margot, like a handsome black moth to a golden flame.

They were so right for each other! Scott and Margot, not Scott and Cherry. And certainly not Scott and Stella Vinton. No!

'Penny for your thoughts,' Scott put in softly, placing his well-kept hand over hers.

Every nerve jumped at the sudden contact, and Cherry gazed down in dismay at the checked tablecloth which she'd been plucking and kneading all the while she reflected on her cousin Margot.

'I'm sorry. I was thinking,' she muttered lamely, and he chuckled.

'That was obvious! But what about, I wonder?' he asked carelessly, still keeping his hand over hers.

Belatedly, she moved her hand, on the pretext of smoothing down the blue and white checked tablecloth. Then the waiter brought their dessert, and the awkward moment was over.

They both chose mousse, and Cherry hurried with hers, not wanting to prolong the lunch. She didn't care to be plied with questions about Cousin Margot. She wanted only to sit and gaze into Scott's deep set eyes, or admire his profile; the straight nose with its slightly flaring nostrils, the firm, almost stubborn chin, that sensuous mouth. Most of all she longed to run her fingers through that thick, glossy black hair.

They had been such good friends once. Almost, but not quite lovers. If the friendship had progressed they would have become lovers, she knew. She loved him and would have held nothing back if by so doing she could make him happy.

Wasn't that true love—wanting to make the one you cared for happy? Yet it had been Scott who cooled the relationship, who had mentally shut her off, Scott who had apparently decided she wasn't what he wanted. And that hurt. But if she could not have him then she hoped he and Margot might belatedly make a go of it. Perhaps in their case absence would make the heart grow fonder.

'Shall we go?' he asked, glancing at his watch, then swearing softly.

'You're late?' Without unnecessary fussing, Cherry gathered her bag and cardigan and hurried out while he settled the bill.

'Not exactly late but cutting it a bit fine,' he admitted, as he emerged into the still-hot day.

She rushed along by his side, part-walking, part-scurrying as she struggled to keep pace. His hand was beneath her elbow, urging her along, and she drew comfort from his nearness. Even though she now realised the past was dead and could not be resurrected, at least she was near to him. A few crumbs of comfort weren't as good as a big meal but they were better than complete starvation, she decided.

They completed the short drive in a tense silence, as though Scott regretted their luncheon engagement, though more than likely his mind was already on his forthcoming afternoon's work.

The big bronze car swept through the hospital gates, coming to rest in the public car-park, a gesture for which Cherry was grateful. The fewer staff who saw her in his car the better.

'Thank you for the lunch—and the lift,' she said briefly, already opening the car door, knowing he would want to take the car around to the parking area reserved for senior staff. He'd spent enough time with her already and she did not want him to be late.

'Cherry.' The way he spoke her name caused her to swing round in astonishment, her eyes wide.

'Yes?' Keeping her voice cool, her eyes hooded, was a struggle but she managed it, not wanting to embarrass him by a display of emotion.

He shrugged, then smiled his lazy half-smile, and her heart turned over. 'Nothing. Let me know about our date on Saturday week, won't you? Leave a note in my pigeon-hole.'

'Oh, but . . .' she began, then smiled briefly and nodded, still keeping her expression neutral. Then she was out of the car and hurrying away without a backward glance.

She wanted to stand and stare until his car was out of sight, wave to him, blow him a kiss. Oh, how she longed to let him see she had missed him, wanted him back! But she must not. Men were easily offended and he would be upset by any display of emotion. She must play down her feelings, keep it cool.

The fact that he still intended taking her out one evening was balm to her mental wounds, though, and with that she had to be content. There was no point in getting excited because he wanted to see her again. She was rather afraid he intended probing her about Cousin Margot.

With that disturbing thought in mind, she headed towards the Nurses' Home, wanting only to reach the privacy of her room so she could have a good cry.

Margot wrote often so Cherry wasn't surprised to receive a letter from her a few days later. Hardly a letter, it was one of the pretty notelets Margot preferred. Her big, sprawling handwriting covered the space and didn't leave much room for detail but that was Margot. Her handwriting matched her extrovert personality and, once more, Cherry wished she could be more like her cousin.

Then perhaps Scott might love *me*, she mused wistfully, as she settled down in her easy chair to read the note. It was her lunch-break and she was still in uniform. It would have to be a quick break because they were busy, as it was Scott's operating day, so she'd purchased a cheese roll from the canteen and taken it back to her room.

She bit into the roll now as she opened the notelet. This one had a picture of a brilliantly plumaged kingfisher on it, she noticed.

She stopped chewing as she read the brief contents. Appetite gone, she carefully put the remainder of the roll back in its cellophane wrapper. Margot was giving a party. Without any real excuse, she confided in the note.

Not that Margot ever needed an excuse, Cherry reflected, her eyes blurring with unshed tears. Margot was kind, always inviting Cherry, always sorry when she could not go.

Or was it because Margot wanted Scott at the parties? Was that the reason she was inviting Cherry now? She knew Scott was at St Monica's, must realise he and Cherry would meet.

She must tell him. He'd wanted to know when Margot was next throwing a party.

Hope gleamed for a moment. If she didn't tell him he would never know. It was virtually certain that Margot would not send him a separate invitation, knowing that Cherry was bound to ask him to accompany her. At Margot's parties one really needed a partner. A lone girl, however attractive, could feel lost in the swirling, noisy mass of Margot's friends.

That was it! She wouldn't tell Scott. All her good resolutions about wanting Scott and Margot to get together vanished. She felt mean and underhand about not telling him but she wasn't actually telling a lie. She was merely omitting to tell the truth.

The ward was in chaos when she returned, there having been a new admission while she was at lunch. Sister Vinton was anxious to go, because she had an urgent dentist's appointment.

Hurriedly she gave Cherry a rundown on the new patient's condition, thrust the notes into her hand and left, her jaw slightly swollen where the offending wisdom tooth was throbbing.

Cherry glanced quickly at the notes. Mrs Edith Cannon, aged fifty-eight. A planned admission because of carcinoma of the vulva, Mrs Cannon had delayed coming in despite the seriousness of her condition.

To arrive at lunch time wasn't ideal but could not be helped. It added to the patient's emotional difficulties, however, and Cherry hastened to meet the woman.

Mrs Cannon wasn't alone and Cherry smiled at the pupil nurse who was chattering away while she helped the patient tidy away her belongings.

Jean Grey, the second-year pupil, was in her early forties, a widow who was doing the job she'd always wanted to do, and Mrs Cannon could not have been in better hands.

'I'm Staff Nurse Mills, Mrs Cannon. Welcome to St Monica's.' Cherry held out her hand and the obese patient held it briefly. Her grip was like a warm jelly, Cherry mused, and her hands were, not surprisingly, sweaty. Coming in was a big decision and the operation was a major one.

Nurse Grey assured Cherry that Sister had seen the patient, she tried to put her at ease, but with the ward being so busy it was virtually impossible, and Cherry left the woman in Nurse Grey's hands, promising to return as soon as she had sorted out the ward.

Scott appeared briefly once she'd brought some order into the chaos. He'd had a busy morning in theatre and was due for an even busier afternoon.

Even casually dressed as he was, in sweat-shirt and cords, he oozed sex-appeal, his heavy-lidded eyes almost caressing Cherry, and she had a hard struggle to keep her love from shining out of her eyes.

Instead, she kept her voice crisp, her attitude strictly professional, and she noticed the atmosphere becoming

visibly cooler, but perhaps it was her over-active im-
agination.

'Bibi seeing Mrs Cannon, is she?' he queried, reading
the notes quickly, and Cherry confirmed that the house
surgeon would be along in about an hour.

'Sister arranged it before she went to the dentist,' she
explained. 'Poor soul has an aching wisdom.'

'Nasty. Ought to be a law against wisdom teeth. Got a
twingeing one myself,' he commented, his expression
grave. 'Left it too late, I think,' he added, tapping the
patient's notes with a blunt forefinger, and Cherry's eyes
darkened with pain.

Knowing Scott would appreciate coffee, she laid it on,
then with a brief apology, hurried back to the patient,
who was now in her nightwear and sitting by her bed
looking extremely unhappy.

Even as Cherry strolled along to sit by her, big tears
started to course down the woman's pudgy cheeks. For a
woman of fifty-eight she looked surprisingly young. Her
colour wasn't good and she was about three stone overweight, but not unattractive.

She had, she assured Cherry, had a cup of tea which
Sister had provided, knowing that a nice cuppa was the
best therapy. She had also been told about the op and
her possible length of stay. Nurse Grey had written
down the visiting times and little snippets about the ward
routine and names of the doctors and nurses, their
uniforms and so on. That last information was important
to the patient even if nurses did not always think so.
They feared to give offence by calling Sister 'Nurse' or
wrongly addressing a senior surgeon. Jean Grey seemed
to have thought of everything.

Cherry couldn't think why Sister Vinton appeared to dislike the woman, confiding to Cherry that Nurse Grey would never pass her State Enrolment, that she was too carefree, not conscious enough of nursing etiquette.

Making the patients comfortable, reassuring them, and performing simple bedside nursing were all that ought to be required of an SEN and Jean Grey filled those needs more than adequately.

Mrs Cannon asked no questions about the operation or her chances of making a complete recovery and Cherry did not broach the subject. It was rarely possible to say there was no hope at all, as Scott had pointed out when discussing Mrs Bailey, and any questions like that must be dealt with according to the consultant's directions.

Her only worry, it transpired, was that she'd left the dog alone. It would be on its own until her daughter arrived during the evening and Mrs Cannon didn't intend giving any of her neighbours a key.

Cherry drew from her the information that she had been widowed for less than a year. Then came more tears, and Cherry was comforting her when their charming Indian housewoman, Bibi, appeared.

Quickly, Cherry organised a nurse to attend the doctor during the examination, then hurried back to the office.

She was waylaid by Anny, the physiotherapist, and was a few seconds too late to say cheerio to Scott Nicholson, with whom Sister Vinton was talking as they strolled towards the door.

Scott turned his head slightly, hearing Cherry's

approach, nodded curtly, then was gone, the doors swinging behind him.

Feeling empty, Cherry forced a bright smile to her lips and was about to commiserate with Sister Vinton on her presumed tooth extraction when something in her senior's gaze stopped her.

Open hostility shone out just for a second, then Stella Vinton shuttered her gaze, and Cherry assumed she had imagined it.

'Mr Nicholson says you want the weekend after next off, Staff Nurse,' Sister said briskly, the starched apron she insisted on wearing rustling crisply as she sat down.

Cherry went white, mentally berating Scott for telling Sister about their dinner engagement.

'Well?' Sister barked, and Cherry quickly recovered her composure.

'Yes please, Sister. But if it isn't convenient, I could make do with just the evening.'

'I generally have weekends, Staff,' Sister pointed out, 'but if you could do the Saturday morning, I'll come on at lunch time and cover the evening. Junior Staff should be on, anyway.'

Surprised at the woman's generosity, Cherry agreed, all the time wondering what Scott had told her.

'Next time do ask, Staff. I don't find it at all pleasant to have consultants asking me if you might have time off. It makes me seem to be an ogre.' Sister's voice was bitter, her gaze sharp, and Cherry silently agreed with her.

'I'm really very sorry, Sister . . .' she began but was waved to silence. Then Sister went on to discuss the new patient and the moment for explanation was over.

Cherry had not intended that Scott should ask for time

off for her. She simply hadn't had a chance to ask Sister herself. He meant well but had done her a disservice.

He was in the canteen the following day when Cherry had an early lunch, not being on duty until twelve-thirty. She never felt like a full meal so early in the day so contented herself with a not very inspiring salad. It was another hot day and the salad looked as limp as Cherry felt.

She would have given anything to be off-duty, preferably stationed somewhere near the swimming-pool, with a large ice-cream.

The canteen was half-empty and she chose a table by the window. Unfortunately she did not see Scott until it was too late. He was sitting with Donald Atkinson at the next table, and Cherry carefully averted her gaze lest he think she was hoping to be invited to join them.

It was the short, portly senior surgeon who saw her first, and he indicated a chair at his table, smiling broadly.

Cherry was about to refuse, especially when she felt another pair of eyes boring into her own. The pale blue eyes stared accusingly at her from under those incredibly thick, black lashes, and she shook her head at Mr Atkinson.

The older consultant would not be denied, however, and before she could protest he'd swept her tray up and was holding the chair for her.

Accepting the inevitable as graciously as she could, Cherry sat opposite Mr Atkinson and next to Scott. So near to Scott, in fact, that her leg accidentally brushed against his thigh as she settled herself.

Flinching from the unexpected contact, she did not

look at him, concentrating instead on pouring mayonnaise on her salad, which now looked even less appetising than it had before.

Mr Atkinson peered at it. 'Not much to look at, is it? I generally have a sandwich.'

'Can't say I blame you, sir,' Cherry said lightly, spearing a portion of tomato. At least the tomato and cucumber were tasty and she could always leave the lettuce.

'Ought to try the salad bar. Shouldn't she, Scott?'

'Yes. Best place in town,' Scott agreed absently, putting down his knife and fork and pushing back his chair. 'Excuse me. Have to dash.'

He was gone before Cherry could really register his presence. Glancing at his plate she saw he hadn't finished his meal. He couldn't bear to sit beside her!

Stifling her disappointment, she kept her eyes on her plate, hoping Mr Atkinson would not indulge in polite conversation. Her hope was in vain.

'About the salad bar—forget what it's called but you get the most marvellous omelette and all the salad you can eat. One of those cut and come again places,' he enthused, his grey eyes kindly, and Cherry forced herself to respond accordingly.

Promising him she would look out for the salad bar, she finished what she could of the salad and rose, glad to go on duty and hoping she wouldn't have to see Scott when she got to the ward.

'I'll take you there, young lady. You might never find it otherwise,' Mr Atkinson was saying. Cherry thanked him, and after a few moments' obligatory conversation, she left.

The fresh air hit her as she walked from the canteen to the main surgical block. Her walk took her across the car-park and she couldn't avoid Scott, who had been at his car. They almost collided, the surgeon putting out a hand to steady her, then snatching it away when he realised who it was.

Hurt, Cherry blurted out, 'Thank you for asking Sister if I might have a weekend off, Scott. That did a lot for my relationship with her! She was really cross.'

He raised a dark brow, eyes unsmiling. There were lines of fatigue around his eyes and mouth, and Cherry had an absurd longing to ease them away, run her fingers across his mouth, down his face . . .

Swallowing the urge was not difficult, for he continued to regard her, his expression stony, eyes cold. 'Since Stella is a friend of mine, I asked her as a favour,' he said, his voice as chilly as his expression. 'She was happy to oblige me. You must have imagined that she was annoyed,' he added, and Cherry gasped at the unfairness of it.

'I did not, but let's forget it, Scott—both the incident and the invitation. Sister is entitled to her weekends and I don't want to upset her. We . . . you have already taken me out for old times' sake,' she added, hoping he might insist that the dinner invitation should stand.

'Please yourself,' was all he said, and Cherry felt about an inch high. He had been kind to her in her first week, trying to ease her into the new hospital, and she'd treated him badly.

By not wishing to appear over-keen, she had gone too far the other way and been offhand, even rude. Scott did not deserve that.

Then she realised how she could make amends. 'Margot!' She said the name with a gasping half-sob, knowing she must tell him of the invitation, yet dreading his acceptance.

He frowned. 'What about her? Is she ill?' He gripped Cherry's wrist, and she opened her mouth in surprise.

'Sorry!' With a rueful smile he released her wrist, then after a quick look around he pulled her towards him and planted a kiss full on her mouth.

His lips burned hers even though the kiss was necessarily a brief one. He released her as suddenly as he'd taken her in his arms, and it was some moments before Cherry could regain her breath.

He seemed as startled as she was, then he gave his slow, sexy smile and Cherry's love shone in her eyes for everyone to see. She wasn't quick enough to stifle the sparkle, the glow that comes from a woman in love, and quickly his smiled faded, his expression becoming set and almost angry.

She bit her lower lip until the pain in her heart eased, then, carefully avoiding his eyes, she told him as briefly as possible about Margot and the party invitation.

She waited with downcast eyes, hoping he would ask if he might accompany her to the party. She had the premonition that, much as he wanted to go, taking her was not on his agenda.

CHAPTER FOUR

THERE was a pause before Scott said quietly, 'Thank you for telling me, Cherry. But Margot sent me an invitation as well.'

'Oh!' Cherry could think of nothing else to say and luckily Scott did not seem to expect any comment, for he patted her shoulder in a fatherly fashion then strode away.

Her sad brown eyes followed his progress until he disappeared through the hospital main doors. Thank you for the silent invitation, Cherry, but it isn't necessary. I'm going anyway. That was the message.

Shaking her head sadly, she walked very slowly to her ward. The invitation from Margot to Scott meant the end of all Cherry's dreams. Margot had decided to make a play for him.

In any case, he didn't want Cherry Mills. He had made that obvious on more than one occasion, she mused as, head bent, she dawdled along, for once not keen to go on duty. That kiss, though. Did it mean anything? She believed not. It was just a kiss to him, a nothingness.

Her lips still burned from it, and would for the rest of the day. She . . .

'How about Monday, Nurse?' Donald Atkinson came puffing up, and Cherry wasn't quick enough to hide the misery in her eyes.

The surgeon gave her a shrewd glance, then repeated

his remark about Monday. 'For lunch at the salad bar I was telling you about. Nice crisp salad. Think of it, Nurse!' he chuckled, and Cherry smiled despite her misery.

'Sounds good!' she countered, lightly.

'Splendid. What time are you free on Monday?'

She hesitated, hardly believing that he meant to take her to lunch. But why shouldn't she go? He was simply being kind to a newcomer. And Scott Nicholson wouldn't care either way.

A time was fixed and surgeon and nurse strolled side by side into the main building. They were the object of a lot of interested looks and remarks, but she no longer cared that word of it might get back to Sister Vinton.

Scott was going to Margot's party by himself. Because he wanted to see Margot again. Where that left Stella Vinton, Cherry wasn't sure. Perhaps he believed there was safety in numbers.

To her own surprise, Cherry accepted Margot's invitation. She would not enjoy the noisy party, making small-talk with people she hardly knew. And she certainly would not enjoy seeing Scott and Margot exchanging fond glances.

No, it was masochism on her part. She recognised that straight away. Or did she harbour the faint hope that she and Scott might travel up together and that he would chose to stay in *her* company all evening?

A couple of weeks before the party she had lunched with Donald Atkinson at the restaurant in Tunbridge Wells. He was right. The salads *were* out of this world, and she enjoyed his undemanding company, too, his gentle humour. They did not talk shop once. He'd told her of his wife's sudden death two years before and of his struggle to gather together the strands of life as a widower.

By and large, he had succeeded. He belonged to several societies and had a large circle of friends. Then there was his work which kept him from brooding. Although so much older than her, they had a lot in common, and Cherry felt unable to refuse when he offered to take her along to a music society meeting when it started up again in October.

The dinner with Scott did not take place. At the last moment she had to cry off because Sister Vinton was unwell and could not exchange duties with her.

Scott hadn't seemed to mind and did not suggest a further date, so it was as well she hadn't set her hopes on it. In a way it was a relief not to go. Having to sit opposite him all evening, making polite conversation and struggling to keep her love hidden, would have been far from easy.

She was settling down into the ward routine now, and there was a steady turnover of patients. Mrs Bailey had been discharged home, to the care of the community nurse but to an uncertain future. Poor Mrs Cannon had died suddenly from a cerebral haemorrhage. Cherry had become fond of the woman, who had tried to be cheerful once the initial strangeness had passed, but it was probably just as well she'd died when she had. They had another patient in now with the same diagnosis, a Mrs Campbell, but the outlook for her was brighter despite her being considerably older.

Now it was the morning of the party, her day off, and

as she struggled out of her lonely bed she put the hospital affairs determinedly from her. She was going to enjoy herself no matter what.

That Scott had made no further mention of the party and had not offered to drive her into London was a blow, but she took it on the chin, refusing to admit that it hurt.

Margot would be able to put her up overnight, then she would get a train back after lunch the next day, which was Saturday—a Saturday she'd been able to get off as the Junior Staff Nurse would be working.

London was well astir by the time Cherry arrived at Margot's big elegant flat, having travelled by train because of a healthy fear of London traffic.

The flat was spacious, occupying the whole of the second floor in an elegant Edwardian mansion set back in a square amid leafy green trees and somewhat grey grass. It was peaceful away from the roar of the traffic and Cherry thought she could be happy there.

How lovely to own the whole house, not just a part. She couldn't bear to think how many servants it would need to be run properly, and dismissed the idea of being the lady of the house as fanciful. A staff nurse's pay wasn't quite enough for a houseful of servants!

Margot, looking as lovely as ever, flung her arms around Cherry and kissed her warmly. Cherry, who didn't care to be kissed by women, family or not, drew back without realising it, and her cousin chuckled.

'Still the same aloof young lady! You can help me sort things out – and wash up afterwards!'

That Margot hadn't already set things out was unusual, and as they prepared the party together Cherry became aware that Margot wasn't her usual self. She was just as noisy, her conversation as lively, but she seemed preoccupied and Cherry sensed a sadness beneath the bright exterior. She was also over made-up, the black mascara did nothing for her beautiful amber eyes, and the dark eyeshadow lent her a rather tired look.

'Not slept well lately?' Cherry said, and Margot started.

'No, no, I haven't. Had a lot on my mind. All six feet of him!' she laughed, and Cherry went cold.

Scott was over six feet tall. Her cousin's remark probably meant nothing but it could be that the extrovert love-'em-and-leave-'em Margot had found true love at last and did not know how to cope with it.

Not wishing to pry, Cherry didn't enquire further. She was afraid Margot might confide in her, and that would be unbearable.

Because she didn't want to wear a dress Scott might remember Cherry had been extravagant and splashed out on a new one.

It wasn't really an extravagance, she assured herself as she changed in the guest room Margot had allocated to her. The dress could be worn again and again, both at hospital functions and during the day. It was leaf-green, a colour that suited her pale blonde looks particularly well, with a square neckline and cap sleeves. Perhaps the colour was too pale for artificial light but she was pleased with it.

Scott probably wouldn't notice what she wore. She was convinced of that when she saw Margot's outfit—a long, paisley-print skirt and a brilliant red blouse with rows of frills down the front. She had the panache to wear such an outfit and look stunning, whereas Cherry

herself would have looked—and felt—ill at ease in such
a bright ensemble.

People began arriving early, generally whole carloads
at a time, and soon the sitting-room and balcony were
crowded, the guests spilling over into bedrooms and
kitchen.

Fortunately the kitchen was large and well-planned,
so there was room enough for guests to wander in and
out as they pleased, without disturbing Cherry, who had
elected to stay behind the scenes preparing sandwiches
and so on. A colleague of Margot's was in charge of the
drinks.

She was busy in the kitchen so did not see Scott arrive,
her first inkling of his arrival being when she turned, a
plate of sandwiches held aloft, only to find Scott with
hand outstretched ready to take the plate from her.

'Oh!' Her bright smile took a few seconds to get going
and it wavered a bit, but on the whole she felt she made a
good job of pretending she was having a great time.

With Scott holding the sandwiches Cherry was able to
keep up a flow of bright, witty conversation while she
opened yet another packet of crisps.

So bright was her conversation that Scott asked
suspiciously if she'd been drinking.

Face flushed, she indignantly denied it, then bit her lip
in annoyance as a rather persistent colleague of Margot's
brought in a bottle and two glasses on a small tray.

'Here we are, Nursie!' Ron Sayers laughed, then
stopped when he saw Scott. 'Should I bring another
glass, Nursie?' he asked, then hiccuped. Scott's lips
tightened.

'Here,' he thrust the plate of sandwiches at Ron, at the

same time taking the tray from him. Without another word, Ron scurried out, and Cherry was about to thank Scott when she saw his set, angry expression.

'I *thought* you'd been drinking,' he said grimly, taking the half-empty bottle and pouring the contents down the sink.

Cherry, who'd had only one pre-party Martini with Margot, protested. Whatever was in the bottle she would gladly have drunk. Certainly with Scott in this censorious mood she needed something!

'I have not been drinking. But I could certainly do with one now!' she snapped, uneasy at his nearness.

'If you persist in skulking in the scullery you won't get a drink!' he smiled. 'The way that lot are knocking it back there won't be any left for the hired help.'

'I am *not* the hired help!' she flared, resenting the implication that that was the reason she had been invited. 'I offered to help out. Margot isn't quite herself,' she added, eyeing him cautiously.

'No, I'd noticed,' he agreed. 'I'll have to go and cheer her up.'

'Yes, you will,' she said forlornly, so forlornly that Scott squeezed her hand.

'Don't be sad. Come and enjoy yourself, Cinders. The night's young.'

Angrily she snatched her hand away, hating him for what she considered his condescending manner. 'Don't call me Cinders! It isn't funny and it isn't clever! I told you, I want to stay out here.'

'No you don't, Cinderella. Come here,' he commanded, and a startled Cherry did as she was bid, her heart beating faster.

His dark head bent towards her and, despite her good resolutions, her lips parted ready for his. Then someone flung the door open, calling for more eats, and hastily they broke apart.

With a sob of frustration, Cherry hurried out with the crisps, calling out to a surprised guest that there were sausages on sticks in the larder if she would fetch them.

Scott followed slowly, probably glad that they had been interrupted, she mused, watching him make a beeline for Margot, who held court at one end of the room.

Margot's tinkling laugh rang out just as Scott got there, and Cherry forced herself to watch as he put an arm about Margot's shoulder, drawing her closer.

The caress was repeated at intervals through the evening, making Cherry feel quite sick. She didn't dare go back to the safety of the kitchen and because the plates and cups were disposable, she didn't even have the excuse of having to wash up.

Instead, she kept as far away as possible from the lovers, as she now thought of them. True, an arm casually about each other could mean nothing, a mere token of friendship probably. But with Scott, it might mean a more serious commitment. He wasn't one to flirt.

Later still, as the crowd thinned out, she spotted the two of them, heads together, as they stood deep in conversation. Then Scott dropped a kiss on Margot's forehead, just as once he'd kissed hers, and Cherry began clearing away vigorously, helped by a rather drunk Ron.

His hands were everywhere but she successfully kept him at bay, never staying in one position long enough for him to touch her except in passing.

'There you are.' She thrust a loaded tray into his eager hands and he looked at it then blinked owlishly, as if not sure what was expected of him.

She turned him in the direction of the open kitchen door, assuring him she would be there shortly, and with a wicked grin, he staggered out with his burden.

If she did have to go into the kitchen she intended making sure she wasn't alone!

Eventually she could put it off no longer. She asked Lena, one of Margot's best friends, to come with her and together they carried in trays of glasses and cutlery. Then Lena was called away, leaving Ron and Cherry alone.

Nervously, Cherry moved away but Ron was quicker and stood with his back to the door, grinning.

'Come and get me, sweetheart!' he offered, and Cherry decided to humour him. She would be unable to fight him off so her best chance was to keep things light, make him laugh if possible.

Laughing, she flung the teatowel at him, telling him he must work for his living if he expected any perks.

Grinning, he eased himself away from the door and was jokingly asking her what he was expected to do with the teatowel when the door was flung open and Scott Nicholson appeared, his face dark with anger.

It was Ron's turn to back away and Cherry almost felt sorry for him. 'We were only having a laugh, honest. Be reasonable. How was I to know she was your girl?' Ron whined.

'I'm not . . . I mean, he and I . . .' Cherry began, but Scott interrupted.

'You know now so I suggest you keep your hands to yourself!' With a dramatic gesture he opened the door wider and ushered out a subdued Ron.

Cherry flushed at the censorious look Scott gave her, even though she wasn't in the wrong.

'Has he been in here long?' Scott demanded, taking a step towards her, and a surprised Cherry explained that until a few moments before Lena had been there.

'Oh.' Slowly he unclenched his fists, struggling for control over his uncertain temper.

Cherry, wondering miserably why he'd told Ron she was his girl, just stood and watched. It was unmistakably Margot who was Scott's girl. She supposed he had rescued her as a kindness, because she was a relative of Margot's. There could be no other reason.

'Are you all right?' he asked belatedly. 'He didn't try anything?'

Cherry smiled vaguely, deliberately so. Let him stew a bit. 'No, no. He's quite nice when you get to know him well.'

His lips tightened, his pale eyes like chips of ice as they bored into her, and she shivered.

Waves of longing swept over her, and it was almost impossible to shut out the attraction, pretend there was nothing between them. The whole room vibrated with an atmosphere she could almost feel. Electric sparks flew back and forth between them, and Scott's eyes were cold no longer.

He moved towards her as if in a dream, her name on his lips. Hardly daring to believe it was happening, that

For that reason she left them alone, pleading a headache, saying that much as she would have liked to join them in the partly-cleared sitting-room, she needed an early night and hoped they wouldn't mind.

Scott rose politely and wished her a goodnight, or what remained of it, his eyes bleak. Margot gave her a hug and thanked her warmly for all her help.

With Margot's perfume lingering in her nostrils, Cherry quietly went to her bed in the spare room. Scott, it transpired, would be sleeping on the bed-settee in the sitting-room.

Cherry lay awake for what seemed hours, listening to the quiet hum of voices, the occasional laugh from Scott. The sitting-room door must be wide open, otherwise I wouldn't hear them, was her last coherent thought before she drifted off.

She could not have slept long before something awakened her. Her first thought was burglars, and she shot up, groping for the light switch.

Then she snatched her hand away, not wanting to warn the intruder. By the luminous dial on the clock she could see that it was three a.m. so she must have slept for almost an hour. Trembling, she lay quietly, listening for the noise again.

Voices. Voices that passed her door on their way to Margot's bedroom. Then Margot's hastily smothered laugh. Silence reigned and Cherry could sleep no longer. It hadn't been an intruder, simply Margot and Scott going to bed. Together? she wondered anew, then soundly berated herself for such a thought.

Dawn found her bleary-eyed, her face wet with tears. Feeling anything but rested she crept out to the bathroom and after a hurried wash went to make herself a cup of coffee. Both Margot's bedroom and the sitting-room doors were tightly closed.

She was drinking her coffee and wondering if she should call Margot when Scott appeared in the kitchen doorway, clad only in a black towelling robe.

Averting her eyes from his bare, muscular legs, Cherry wished him a cheery good morning and poured him a cup of coffee. She wondered, briefly, which room he'd slept in. He had certainly come through from the sitting-room, and it was none of her business, anyway.

But it *is* my business! she cried silently, as she slipped some thick slices of bread under the grill. I love the man! I need to know where I stand.

Scott ran long, sensitive fingers through his thick hair as she turned back to him. 'Thought I would give you a lift back, Cherry. If you want one, that is?'

His tone was polite but a smile lurked in the depths of those heavy-lidded eyes, and Cherry found herself responding to the warmth she found there.

'Oh yes, please! I'm not in any hurry to get back, though. Junior Staff Nurse is in charge,' she explained.

'I'm off, too. How about taking the long route home? Taking in a bit of seaside while we're doing it?'

'The way to Tunbridge Wells isn't via the seaside!' she laughed. 'But it will make an interesting diversion.'

Pleased that he actually wanted to take her back with him, she was humming a little tune as she buttered the toast. She could feel his eyes upon her, and her face and body grew heated at the thought of she and Scott together in their very own kitchen, rising after a warm night spent in each other's arms! How wonderful that would be, she mused, her smile wistful as she waited on Scott.

Margot spoiled the dream by drifting in on a cloud of perfume, already dressed, to Cherry's surprise. Margot chuckled at her expression. 'I heard Scott so thought I would be ladylike and dress. I'll shower later. Coffee smells good.'

She flashed Scott a brilliant smile and patted his arm affectionately.

Cherry, seeing the loving gesture, busied herself putting out another cup and saucer.

'Did Scott tell you about driving you home?' Margot asked, and Cherry drew in her breath sharply.

'Why, yes,' she admitted, after a moment's hesitation. 'He very kindly offered.'

'Wasn't it a good idea of mine? Save you a train journey,' Margot carried on, but Cherry closed her ears after that.

It was Margot's idea, not his. *He* didn't want to take her back to St Monica's. Margot had persuaded him.

Cherry felt sick and very, very cold. Symptoms of shock, she told herself firmly. Get a grip on yourself, girl. The world isn't coming to an end just because Scott doesn't care for you any more. Forget him. Life goes on.

Yet life without Scott, she now realised, wasn't life at all. It was a mere pretence, a going through the motions of living.

She could not refuse Scott's offer of a lift, even though it would be unbearable sitting beside him, knowing he was merely driving her back to oblige Margot.

Yet, it was a lovely summer's morning and Cherry's

spirits rose briefly as they headed out of London, and
once they were on the road to Tunbridge Wells, she
relaxed, unclenching her fists, closing her eyes and
letting the warmth of the sun drive out the shadows.

'After Tunbridge Wells I thought we might make a
detour down to the coast. Fancy Margate? Or further
on? Somewhere quieter, perhaps?' Scott's voice broke
into her muddled thoughts, disturbing the fragile peace,
and she frowned, her expressive eyes hidden behind
enormous sun-glasses.

'No, I don't think so. I have a headache coming.' That
wasn't really a lie. She probably would have one by the
time they reached St Monica's. 'Could we go straight to
Caldergate, do you think?' she pleaded, not wanting to
prolong the agony.

'Yes, if you wish,' he said stiffly, and she almost
groaned. Now she had offended him and he was simply
being kind.

'I don't want you to feel obliged to take me back,' she
said suddenly. 'I mean—if you want a day at the seaside
you could drop me off somewhere.'

What had made her say that she didn't know. But she
was annoyed when he seemed to consider the idea.
'Might do that. I certainly don't fancy Caldergate that
much,' he mused aloud, slowing the car as they neared a
lay-by.

It was empty except for a heavy lorry parked some
yards away, and apparently it was miles from habitation,
for all around Cherry's puzzled gaze took in fields and
hedgerows—and sheep. Thousands of sheep.

Over to their right the river sparkled in the sun, and
traffic hurtled by on the busy road as they stopped.

'There. This suit you?' he asked genially, sliding an arm along the back of the seat as he turned towards her.

Taking off her sun-glasses, she gave him a searching glance, wondering if the hot sun had proved too much for him. 'It's the back of beyond, Scott,' she pointed out. If it was a joke she did not see the funny side of it.

'Hardly. The river is over there,' he murmured. 'See?' Putting out a lean hand he turned her face in the direction of the river, and she trembled.

'Yes. Thank you. I've already seen it!' she flared, struggling to free herself but failing.

'If you don't want water there are plenty of sheep to look at,' he went on, conversationally. 'And we passed a couple of horses in a field a mile or so back. You could always stroll back that way and offer them a piece of apple.'

He was smiling now, that wicked half-smile she knew so well. He was laughing at her, perhaps not visibly, but he was obviously enjoying every minute.

Tears pricked her eyelids as he dropped his hands to her shoulders, squeezing her gently.

'Cherry—look at me,' he whispered, his voice soft and seductive. It was the old trap and one she wasn't going to fall into.

Refusing to do as she was bid, she closed her eyes and waited for him to turn from her.

Instead, his fingers began a slow, seductive exploration of her body, starting with her eyelids, trailing sensuously down her cheek and pausing at her mouth, which he outlined with one finger, even though she still stubbornly refused to look at him.

Then his hand was at her throat, and she tried to

control the delicious quivering sensation that shot right through her body, but she wasn't entirely successful, for he chuckled, that husky chuckle that made her toes curl with desire.

'Scott, stop it,' she breathed. 'You have no right!'

His hands were still for an instant; then moved down. His arm settled about her slender waist where his touch did her blood pressure no good at all.

With his thumb, he caressed her breast through the thin material of her pretty sun-dress, and she pulled away, her eyes snapping open. She couldn't let him take such liberties. Not now, when she knew his heart belonged to Margot.

'Don't do that!' she exploded, her hand raised as if to strike him, but he only chuckled and she lowered her arm, ashamed that she had so nearly hit him, an act alien to her gentle nature. Margot had a lot to answer for!

'You used to like being stroked,' he whispered, putting an arm about her again and drawing her closer, despite her protests.

'That was before—' she wailed, then stopped, horrified at what she had so nearly said.

'Before what? Mm?'

'Before . . . before you left,' she prevaricated.

'I see.' His tone was strange, withdrawn even, and he released her, settling back on his own side of the car and setting it into motion.

Feeling cold and bereft, Cherry leant back in the comfortable seat and stared straight ahead, trying to pretend the whole episode had never happened.

Yet her body ached for his stroking caress, her lips yearned to be kissed. It could never be. Not now. He was amusing himself with her, toying with her like a cat with a mouse, enjoying it when she tried to escape, knowing there could never be an escape from him.

She loved him and that was all there was to it. But she was going to take great care that he never found out.

Let him believe it was merely a strong physical attraction. That way she might salvage her pride, if not her heart.

CHAPTER FIVE

SISTER Vinton shot her a sharp glance. 'Have you been listening, Staff Nurse?' she enquired silkily, and Cherry flushed.

'No. I haven't, Sister. I'm sorry,' she admitted, believing it best to be honest. If she was asked to repeat what Sister had been telling her she could not do so.

Sister pursed her lips, an ugly gesture, Cherry thought. And an ageing one. Stella Vinton looked nearer forty than thirty this morning, but perhaps her weekend had been as terrible as Cherry's own.

'I was discussing the linen situation,' Sister went on briskly. She did not repeat what she had already said about it but Cherry gathered that matters were going from bad to worse regarding laundry.

'Now they're foisting these housekeeping teams on us!' Sister's voice broke in on Cherry's jumbled thoughts again. If they had been discussing patients she would have been all attention but linen hardly mattered on a grey, rainy day with low clouds upon her own horizon as well as in the sky.

'Perhaps they might be a good idea?' she ventured, only to be quelled by a look.

'They might, just might, save us a bit of time,' Sister conceded. 'But they will need supervising. And heaven knows we can't always be behind them!' Still grumbling, Sister rustled away, leaving a weary Cherry to gaze at the near-empty shelves in the linen cupboard. Empty when they ought to be nearly full.

Problems, problems. If it wasn't the staff causing problems, it was the patients. Or the domestics. In this case it was the laundry. Ward sisters ordered their own supplies from the linen store but just lately there never seemed enough to go around. At one stage Sister told her they had been reduced to using paper sheets because of industrial unrest at the hospital laundry.

Now it was being suggested that special housekeeping teams should work on the wards, such as were already seen in many hospitals. They would relieve the sisters of many of the routine tasks that could be better performed by non-nurses, leaving the senior nursing staff to carry out the tasks for which they were trained.

Cherry believed this to be an excellent idea, but Sister thought otherwise, and Cherry really did not have the heart to argue with her.

It would only be an academic argument. Whether they wanted them or not, the first housekeeping team would arrive on Turner ward the following morning.

'Mr Nicholson should be here but he isn't.' Sister was still grumbling when Cherry walked into the office. She halted, her nerves on edge.

'Should he be? Why? It isn't his round.'

'No, but I particularly wanted to see him. He promised to look in some time this morning and there is that meeting I have to attend.'

When Cherry remained silent, Sister glanced up. 'Did you hear me? You will have to go instead.'

It would be better than waiting on the ward for Scott anyway, and Cherry was pleased at the thought. 'Is it a meeting about the housekeeping teams, Sister?'

'No. It's a policy committee meeting. There won't be any need for you to say anything. Just sit quietly and listen. Make a few notes if you like. Here.' Sister handed her the agenda and Cherry scanned it briefly.

As Sister had said, it was simply a meeting, one of the dozens of meetings that took place in the hospital every month. Anyway, she would be glad to be off the ward when Scott came.

'Why is Mr Nicholson coming, Sister? Is it something special?'

Sister Vinton went red, and Cherry could have bitten out her tongue. Evidently it was a personal matter.

'It's private, Staff Nurse,' Sister confirmed, without meeting Cherry's gaze. 'There may be good news on the way,' she added, opening some of the casenotes and bending her head over them.

Cherry's lips tightened. Sister could be annoyingly vague when she wanted to be. And if Stella Vinton reckoned on a future shared with Scott Nicholson she was going to be a disappointed woman. For now he'd met Margot again no other woman would get a look-in.

If any good news was imminent, it would come from Margot and Scott—together. With sinking heart, Cherry fetched her cloak and trudged off to the meeting, knowing that when the announcement came she could not continue at St Monica's.

The meeting was short and, to Cherry's mind, inconclusive, a sheer waste of nursing and medical staff time. It was all right for the admin. people. It was part of their job to attend meetings, add more bits of paper to their already cluttered desks, but she did not think Sister would appreciate the sheaf of notes she was bringing back for her.

The only interesting part of the meeting was that Donald Atkinson also attended, coming in half-way through. He made straight for Cherry, seating himself next to her with a beaming smile to which she found herself responding.

He was distinguished-looking, she mused, glancing at him out of the corner of her eye. Not much more than five feet five or six, and on the heavy side, but his silvery hair gave him an air of distinction and he was always immaculately dressed. Just like Scott.

Angry with herself for thinking about Scott, who already had two women in tow, Cherry forced her attention back to the meeting, which appeared to be coming to a close, thank goodness.

Mr Atkinson leaned towards her as the chairman declared the meeting closed, his sleeve accidentally brushing her bare arm. 'How about meeting me on your next day off, Cherry?'

It was the first time he'd used her Christian name. Even when he'd taken her to the salad bar he had been careful to address her only as Staff Nurse. This was a new development and one Cherry wasn't sure she could handle.

She turned sad, weary eyes upon him, and he chuckled. 'You look like the morning after the night before! Had a bad weekend?'

She nodded and smiled. 'A very bad weekend. I went to a party but everything went wrong,' she confessed, surprising herself by telling him. She mustn't do that. It wasn't fair to embroil a near-stranger in her personal affairs.

'Are you free Friday evening?' He did not elaborate, so she wasn't sure what the invitation entailed.

Friday was her day off, as it happened. Or ought to have been, but Sister had asked her to work until lunch time.

'Yes, I'm free after lunch,' she admitted, wondering how she was to refuse if he was inviting her to dinner. She really could not cope.

But it wasn't an intimate dinner for two, and she relaxed when he told her it was a party.

'A better party than the one you've recently endured, I hope!' he laughed.

They walked back together, talking amicably. Just before they parted company he told her a joke against himself, and she was still smiling when she swept through the swing-doors of the ward. It was a smile that rapidly faded when she saw Scott and Sister in the office.

Sister was at her desk with Scott leaning over her. Their heads were close together and they were laughing quietly at some private joke.

Cherry's mouth dropped open in astonishment, then Scott glanced up, that lazy smile lingering on his lips.

'Good morning, Staff Nurse. I hope you had a good weekend?'

Cherry recovered her composure and told him that she'd had a rotten weekend, thank you sir, and his eyes narrowed.

Sister frowned at her but Cherry was beyond caring. 'And did *you* have a pleasant weekend, Mr Nicholson?' she asked sweetly, her eyes blazing defiance at him.

'Yes, very fruitful,' he murmured, then smiled at Sister before striding out, his jaw set.

To get out of the office he had to pass Cherry, who stepped aside quickly. But not quickly enough to miss the hissed aside from the surgeon, 'I'll see you later!'

With that, he was gone, leaving only the faintest aroma of aftershave, and Cherry felt sick, realising she had gone too far.

What retribution would he exact for her insolence? she wondered, as she went to check on the patients.

They actually had a vacancy now, a rare occurrence, but a new admission was due the next day, a patient who had telephoned Scott's secretary every day, asking when she was to be admitted. Cherry hoped the woman, Mrs Chamberlayne, would be happier once the operation was over. It seemed from advance information that she was suffering a lot of discomfort and a great many vague symptoms.

There must be a change-over of beds, Cherry decided. Sister usually left that sort of thing to her, being more concerned with the consultant's rounds and the various committees she attended.

Mrs Chamberlayne must be nearest the office, a position Miss Westerman occupied now. She would be discharged, probably after Scott's next round, but in the meantime she could go to the other end.

With bedding list in hand, Cherry walked the length of the ward, making notes as she went and stopping to talk to each patient. The ladies did not like to be moved, as a rule. They made friends with others in the four-bedded cubicles, and it unsettled them to be placed in a different group. Of course eventually they settled down, if they had time before discharge, but Cherry didn't like to move them if at all possible.

Miss Westerman was glad to be moved, however. She confided to Cherry that she didn't care for the others in her group, making Cherry bend down so that she could whisper in her ear.

Her voice had a carrying quality, though, and there were suppressed giggles from the other beds.

Miss Westerman was in her late sixties and the others were all quite a bit younger, so it was hardly surprising she was keen to move. Cherry arranged for her to be moved two groups farther down, where she might fit in better.

When she had finished altering the bedding-list, Cherry went in search of Jean Grey, the pupil nurse.

Mrs Skelton, their new auxiliary, indicated the sluice with a vague gesture, and Cherry sighed. She would have to speak to the woman when she had more time, point out that jerking a thumb in the required direction wasn't the way to behave towards her seniors. If she did that in Scott's presence, he would be furious.

She found Pupil Nurse Grey in one of the bathrooms, which were just off the sluice. Her normally cheery face was wet with tears, and Cherry halted uncertainly. If she was having a good cry it wasn't fair to disturb her. The bed-moving wasn't urgent.

Jean Grey saw Cherry before she could dodge back. Hastily scrubbing at her face, she said, 'Can I help you, Staff? I . . . I was cleaning the bath. Mrs Jones had one and I—'

'It's all right, Jean. It will keep.' Cherry hesitated, then plunged on, 'If I can do anything, do tell me. A shoulder to cry on sometimes helps,' she smiled.

Jean smiled back, then blew her nose. 'There. That's better. It just comes on me sometimes, Staff Nurse. She . . . Sister, that is, she's so finicky at times. And she ticked me off in front of that boyfriend of hers.'

'Boyfriend?' Cherry echoed, and the nurse nodded vigorously.

'Mr Nicholson. He and Sister are – well, like that.' She crossed her fingers, and Cherry nodded. 'You know they were almost engaged once?' the nurse went on, and Cherry hesitated before agreeing that she had known that.

'Well, they even went shopping for the ring. Sister set her heart on a big sapphire. My friend told me, because it was before I came on to this ward,' Jean confided, setting her cap straight.

Cherry, numb, could only stand and listen. She was aware that she ought to reprimand the nurse, tell her firmly that she should not be gossiping about Sister behind her back, but she could not. She wouldn't have been human if she hadn't wanted to learn all she could about Stella Vinton's relationship with Scott, so she let the woman continue.

Why the engagement fell through, Jean didn't know. Her friend believed they had quarrelled, but had made it up now and were as fond of each other as ever.

'She even stays at his house when she's off-duty,' Jean confided, and Cherry's heart went plummetting to her lace-up shoes.

'I really think we should get on, Jean,' Cherry said at last. 'We ought not to be discussing Sister's love-life,' she added firmly, aware that she was more at fault than the pupil nurse. She must discourage all the nurses from discussing Sister's private life.

For the rest of the day she couldn't get Jean's words out of her mind. Sister and Scott were almost at the stage of buying the ring but something had stopped them.

Where did that leave poor Margot? she wondered. If he and Sister were as thick as ever then he was raising Margot's hopes unnecessarily. Cherry was fond of her attractive cousin despite their different personalities, and could not stand idly by while Scott broke Margot's heart as well as her own.

Yet, what could she do? That was the problem—but Scott solved it for her.

He accosted her as she left the ward that evening, having been on a split duty. She'd had to stay late even then, because the condition of one of the patients was causing anxiety. It was nearly ten o'clock by the time she emerged from the side door and paused, wondering if she should take the short-cut across the car-park.

It was a dark cloudy evening and one never knew. Perhaps it would be safer to go out by the main entrance.

Looking back, she thought it a pity she'd changed her mind, because Scott was waiting for her when she re-traced her steps.

'You're late,' he said briefly, grasping her by the upper arm and leading her towards the side entrance from which she had just come.

'Will you let me go!' she hissed, as he hurried her along. The corridors were empty now and she repeated her demand, louder this time, but got no response.

'Scott! I'm tired. I want to go home!' she wailed, but although his painful grip eased a little he did not release her.

'I'm tired, too. I've had an exceptionally busy day, but I came back to talk to you.'

'What about Mrs McNiven? We were worried. That's why I'm late,' she panted as she struggled to keep pace with his long legs.

'I know about her. My senior registrar was there, wasn't he?'

'Yes, but . . .'

'He is perfectly capable of making a decision. If he's worried he knows where he can contact me. Geoff's looking for his first consultancy post so he can't come running to me every five minutes,' he added, guiding her towards his car.

She hung back, afraid. 'I want to go to bed, Scott. I've had a busy day, as well. Can't we talk tomorrow?' she wailed, then caught her breath sharply as she was almost pushed into the front seat of the car.

'Tomorrow may be even busier. I have more important things to do, anyway,' he finished, unkindly, and Cherry clenched her fists.

Tears were not far away and his words caught her below the belt. He had more important matters to attend to than talk to Staff Nurse Mills. Though once that had not been the case.

Memories of what once had been crowded into her mind and she put up no further resistance. If he wanted to tell her off, even report her for what he might consider insolence, it did not seem to matter any more.

He drove in silence, and after a while she roused

herself to glance out into the night. It was certain they weren't going to the Nurses' Home and equally certain that they were not on the way to Caldergate.

A sign flashed by and Cherry's eyes widened. They were on the road to London!

'Scott!' She clutched at his sleeve, causing him to stifle an oath. 'Where are we going? I demand to know!' Agitated, she turned on him fiercely, uncaring that they were going at a fair speed.

'For God's sake woman, simmer down!' he thundered. 'Do you want to cause an accident? We're going to my home, so we can talk,' he explained, his tone sharp and brooking no argument.

'Your home?' With a sigh she settled back, arms folded defensively. All she wanted was sleep and he was taking her to his home, which must be miles from the hospital. Men!

Scott lived in a quiet, tree-lined drive, a drive so badly-lit that Cherry knew she would not be able to recognise it again. His house was right at the end, on its own and hidden behind a tall hedge.

He drove carefully up the short drive, then switched off the engine. In the ensuing silence Cherry's heartbeat sounded unnaturally loud to her ears.

Instead of getting out, Scott relaxed, letting his hands with their slender, sensitive fingers rest lightly on the steering-wheel.

'Well?' she demanded. 'Have we come all this way just so I can sit here and freeze? I'm tired!' she exploded, her nerves shot to pieces by his very nearness.

'Will you be quiet!' He turned on her fiercely, and she flinched away. 'Come on. Let's go into the house.' With

a sudden movement he reached across her to undo her
door, and she shrank back against the seat, afraid lest his
arm should accidentally brush against her breasts.

He chuckled, and Cherry's face burned. She was glad
of the all-enveloping darkness to hide her embarrassment as she followed him to the big heavy door set within
a covered porch.

'Welcome to my abode, Staff Nurse!' He waved a
hand in the general direction of what she supposed was
the sitting-room, and hesitantly she ventured into the
wide hallway, her feet sinking into the deep pile of the
peacock-blue carpet. She went into the room he'd indicated, to find more of the same coloured carpet, which,
despite its brightness, blended well with the muted tones
of the furnishings.

Surprised at the lack of furniture, she sat on the edge
of the grey velvet settee. The settee was the main item of
furniture, together with its attendant armchairs and a big
matching wing-chair by the log-effect electric fire. Apart
from that, all Scott had in the room was a coffee table
and a wall unit.

Curtains of cream velvet completed the scene,
together with cushions to match. A water-colour paint-
ing was set low on one wall. There was a portable
television in the corner, but she doubted if he viewed
very often. Scott had never been one to sit entranced in
front of the box.

'Coffee won't be a minute.' Scott emerged from
another door which she supposed led to the kitchen.
With a weary sigh he flopped into the wing-chair and
crossed his long legs. 'Good to be home,' he commented, when Cherry didn't speak.

'Yes, it would be,' she said acidly, causing Scott to give her a sharp look.

'Thought you would like to see how I lived,' he murmured, leaning forward to plug in the fire. 'You always were a great one for the domestic scene,' he added, and Cherry bit her lip in annoyance.

'Women are always interested in houses, in how others live,' she defended herself, and a slow smile spread across his handsome face. Cherry reddened and gazed down at the carpet beneath her feet.

He was sniping at her because during their brief courtship she'd always been looking in the windows of furniture shops or drapers, gazing entranced at rows of curtains hanging in one shop, or eagerly trying out armchairs in another.

It was unfair to laugh at her. Unfair and unkind, and she told him so. 'You've always had a home, Scott. Your own bed, your own room, little treasures around you. Things you take for granted,' she said quietly. 'You know my parents were killed when I was sixteen. After that I lived in lodgings until I started nursing.'

Her voice was low, so low that he had to lean forward to catch the words. 'You can't blame me for wanting a home of my own one day. Even if it's only a one-bedroom flat.'

She hesitated before mentioning the most painful point of all, perhaps the main cause of Scott's subsequent coldness. 'I . . . I didn't intend you to think that I . . . that I had marriage in mind!' she blurted out, avoiding his eyes. 'Just because I like looking at items for the home, it doesn't mean I was trying to trap you! "Trying to land a prize fish", as you once put it!' In her indignation she met his gaze at last, her brown eyes sparking fire at him.

Pity was etched on his face, in his blue eyes, for all to see and suddenly she hated him. She didn't want his pity. She wanted his love!

She fought down the urge to hurl herself at him, an action which would have been alien to her nature.

'You could always rent a little place,' he pointed out quietly, but she shook her head.

'It wouldn't be the same. I want a place of my own.' She didn't add that even then she would not be satisfied. A house was just so much bricks and mortar. To be happy a house should be filled with people—and love. She needed someone to share that little house one day. Until then she would carry on saving for it and continue to live in the Nurses' Home. Conditions were not ideal there but at least they were free of the petty restrictions that learners had to endure.

They could have men in as long as they were out by midnight—could even have them in their rooms if they wished. There was no Home Warden in that part of the Home to decree otherwise. Male staff, too, lived in the Home and were often to be met with in the kitchen, hoping some kind female would cook them a free breakfast to save them going over to the canteen! At the moment there were few staff in that section and Cherry found it rather lonely.

Why, Scott had even visited her room, she recalled, her face growing warm as she remembered the scene. She had been so frightened that he meant to kiss her passionately. And all he did was drop a light kiss on her brow instead of upon her eager mouth!

Perhaps Scott had been right to run away from her. Maybe her pursuit had frightened him. Yet she had never meant it so. If she could not have his love she would try to be content with his friendship. She had never expected a brilliant budding consultant to consider marrying a newly-qualified staff nurse as she'd been then. Scott could do far better for himself.

Tired of her own thoughts, she glanced across at the object of them. He was asleep, worn out by his arduous day.

Cherry's fingers itched to smooth away the lines from his brow and mouth. She longed to undo his tie and slip off his shoes so that he might be more comfortable.

Yet she must not touch him, lest he think she was pursuing him, trying to rush him up the aisle. Men liked to make the running. All she had hoped for in coming to St Monica's was to be near, if and when he decided to pursue her!

But it seemed that cousin Margot and Sister Vinton both had prior claims on him.

She closed her eyes, the glow from the electric fire illuminating her sad face as she slept.

CHAPTER SIX

WHEN Cherry awoke from her brief doze it was to find herself covered by a large tartan rug. She sat up, uncertain where she was for a moment. The room was unfamiliar.

Then she remembered it was Scott's home. The electric fire was drying the atmosphere and she got up to switch it off. She was alone but from the next room there came a tuneless whistling and the rattle of crockery.

Embarrassed because she'd fallen asleep in his house she wandered out to the kitchen and paused in the doorway, as yet unseen by Scott, who was pouring out two cups of coffee, one with very little milk which she knew was for her.

Cherry's heart ached because of the cosy domesticity of the scene, a scene of which she could never be part.

She must have made some sound, a sigh perhaps, for he swung around, his expression unfathomable. 'Do you want a biscuit? There's loads of them in the barrel.'

Smiling a little, Cherry put a few of the biscuits on a plate. Chocolate biscuits, most of them. Scott's favourites. Tears welled up behind her eyes and she hurried back to the sitting-room with the plate.

'I'm sorry I fell asleep, Scott,' she murmured, stirring her coffee, her head bent over the cup to avoid his gaze.

'It doesn't matter. I had a cat-nap, too. It's been a long day,' he commented, and Cherry took it to mean that he was too tired to drive her back to the hospital. Well, she would ring for a taxi. She could understand his reluctance to leave the warm, cosy little house. A home.

She lifted her head but still avoided looking in his direction. Her pensive gaze took in the comfort and understated elegance of the furniture, the velvet curtains which she would have liked in her room at St Monica's, the rich colour of the carpet.

She swallowed the lump which rose into her throat, and told Scott how much she admired the sitting-room. Casting a quick glance at him she saw his eyes were almost closed as he lay back in the wing-chair.

'Sort of place you fancy, I suppose?' he said idly, and Cherry wished she hadn't spoken.

'No, not exactly,' she hastened to tell him, and his eyes shot open.

He frowned. 'What's wrong with it? I thought it was comfortable, not too showy.' He sounded affronted, and Cherry gazed fixedly at the rapidly cooling coffee.

In the silence she could hear the loud ticking of the clock set high on the wall above his head. She saw that it was nearly midnight.

'Heavens!' She jumped up, spilling the dregs of her coffee over her uniform. 'I'm on early shift tomorrow!' she told the startled Scott, as she ineffectually dabbed at the coffee stain. It was probable that the laundry would be able to fade the stain but she ought to wash it off before it set. She couldn't do so now. It would have to wait until she got back to St Monica's.

'Here. Give it to me. I'll soak it in the bath.' To her astonishment, Scott, after waiting a few seconds for the message to sink in, calmly unzipped the dress and drew it over her head. She was left standing in her new pink slip.

He was out of the room with the dress before Cherry could collect her scattered wits. Her face burned, and she wrapped herself in the tartan rug to await his return, her thoughts in turmoil.

Scott came whistling downstairs after a few minutes, holding out the uniform so Cherry could see the damp patches where he'd sponged out the stain. 'Shouldn't be too bad now. Is it too damp to wear?'

She didn't want to let go of the rug which needed both hands to hold it on. 'No, that's fine,' she muttered, cursing him as he held out the dress for her to take.

Realising that she must take it from him, she reached for it, losing her grip on one side of the rug, leaving her arms and one leg bare.

'For God's sake, Cherry!' he exploded, tearing the rug from her grasp and tossing it on the floor. 'Why all this maidenly modesty! I haven't got designs on your virtue!' he snapped, thrusting the damp dress into her arms. He slammed into the kitchen, leaving a tearful Cherry to dress.

Not only was she embarrassed, she was heartbroken too. He hadn't got designs on her. Well, she knew that, but did he have to be so brutal about telling her? Of course she did not expect him to become excited over a scantily-clad female. To a surgeon a body was probably just a collection of organs, some with more interesting symptoms than others.

Carefully, she folded the rug and laid it over the back of the armchair. Then she slipped her shoes on again and zipped up the dress.

There, now she would telephone for a taxi since Scott

was sulking in the kitchen. The phone must be in the hall, and she wandered out. It was much cooler out there and it gave her overheated face and body a chance to cool off.

'What are you doing now?' Scott's exasperated voice halted her as she was about to dial the local taxi service.

'I'm ringing for a taxi,' she said crisply, trying to pretend she was on duty. Trying to forget that little incident, as well.

He snatched the receiver from her and banged it down on its rest. 'I'll drive you home, Cherry. I can't send you back in a taxi at this time of night.'

He sounded weary as indeed he must be, and Cherry's heart went out to him. 'Please, Scott. Don't worry about me. The taxi will take me right to the Nurses' Home entrance. You're tired,' she finished quietly.

She put her hand on his, trying to convey her sympathy, unprepared for the violence with which he thrust her away.

'Don't play with me, Cherry! This cool-one-minute, warm-the-next act is getting me down!' His voice was harsh, strained, and her eyes widened with shock.

This wasn't the cool, controlled Scott Nicholson she knew! His eyes were tormented, filled with the cold passion that Staff Nurse Hedy Graham had once described, and Cherry backed away, wondering what danger she had unleashed.

Scott gave a wry smile. 'I won't drag you screaming off to bed, Cherry! It wouldn't be professional, would it? I'll get my jacket.'

He walked back to the kitchen, Cherry's stricken gaze following him. Just what she'd expected she didn't know. Certainly not that display of temper—of raw passion. For that was what she'd seen in his eyes.

Scott wanted her. She still mattered to him, but in what way? As a convenient and readily available substitute for the glamorous Margot, she supposed as, with heavy heart, she silently followed him to the car.

The ward was even busier than usual the rest of the week, for which Cherry was glad. She didn't want time to think, to brood on Scott's attitude. One thing she knew, if he was truly in love with Margot she herself would keep well out of his way. Whatever he might feel for her it certainly wasn't love, as his behaviour on Monday night had demonstrated—Cherry Mills would do if no one else was available.

Cherry's blood boiled at the thought. He was no better than a philanderer! Yet it was out of character. Scott wasn't like that. He did not play the field, collect women's hearts like a scalp-hunter collecting scalps. Perhaps the truth lay somewhere in between. He liked herself, Margot and Stella, but did not love any of them.

Poor Margot evidently believed he *did* love her and Cherry wanted to protect her cousin, believing that Margot was in love for the very first time and could not handle the emotion. She had always considered Margot shallow, caring only for her own selfish pleasures, and it was a salutary lesson to learn that even the glamorous Margot had tender feelings.

'We've a Mrs Lewin coming in,' Sister's loud voice dragged Cherry away from her bitter introspection, and she was glad.

'An emergency, Sister?' Cherry frowned, knowing they had no records for the woman.

'No, but Mr Nicholson wants her in next,' Sister explained, throwing a folder down on to the desk.

She looked tired, dispirited, and Cherry briefly wondered if her love-life was going badly. Apart from on his round, Scott hadn't been near the ward, leaving as much as possible in the capable hands of his senior registrar.

Cherry opened the folder as Sister rustled out, muttering 'laundry' to herself as she went.

The burden of being a ward sister! Cherry knew she had sufficient experience to apply for such a post but wasn't at all sure she wanted to. Hard as it was to be a staff nurse, it would be harder as a sister, with all the decision-making that it involved. Far less interesting, too, as sisters did not do so much bedside nursing.

Shrugging, Cherry read the admission details. Mrs Pam Lewin would be arriving just after lunch according to the note pinned to the folder—a note written by Scott.

Scott! All roads led to him and, not for the first time, Cherry wished she hadn't left London.

'Ah, you've got them.' Scott materialised from out of nowhere and neatly plucked the folder from Cherry's hands.

Settling himself in Sister Vinton's chair, he crossed his legs and immersed himself in his reading, leaving an annoyed Cherry to drum her fingers on the desk.

'What do you think?' he asked suddenly, laying his strong hand over hers to stop her from fidgeting.

She jumped, and his eyes narrowed in surprise. 'I never realised you had such bad nerves, Cherry. Think you should see your GP?' he enquired mildly, and Cherry's eyes sparked fire at him.

Then he chuckled and she flushed, feeling foolish because she hadn't seen that it was a joke.

'Sorry. I forgot you take everything so seriously,' he said, and she wondered if she should take that remark as a joke as well.

'I can't tell you what I think,' she said primly, 'because I haven't read the notes yet.'

His head jerked up, the good humour leaving him. 'Why haven't you read them? I sent them up a good hour ago!'

Her lips tightened. How she hated scenes. 'They haven't been on the ward for a good hour, Mr Nicholson,' she said firmly, meeting his accusing gaze. 'Sister brought them in only a few moments before you came in and . . . and snatched them back!'

They glared at each other. The air was thick with electric sparks just as Donald Atkinson breezed in.

'Oh!' He held up his arms as if he were being held at gunpoint, and Cherry smiled tightly at him.

Scott, however, did not smile as he curtly acknowledged the other surgeon. He rose, then flung Mrs Lewin's notes down on the desk. 'Read them,' he said flatly, then strode out, leaving Cherry staring after him, the older surgeon all but forgotten.

Donald Atkinson snapped his fingers and Cherry focused on him at last. She hadn't meant to be rude but the scene with Scott had taken its toll. She shivered as she met Donald's kind grey eyes.

'Thought I'd confirm the time. For the party,' he said, as Cherry gazed at him, perplexed.

'Yes. The party. When is it?' She passed a hand across her eyes, a hand that trembled, then smiled tremulously at the consultant.

He frowned. 'Get a hold on yourself, Staff Nurse!' His tone was sharp and it brought Cherry back from the chilly nether world she'd been occupying. It was just what she needed.

'I'm sorry, Mr Atkinson. I'm all right now,' she assured him, the casenotes clutched defensively to her chest.

'Sure?'

'Mm. I'm sure. We . . . Mr Nicholson and I had a disagreement. Over nothing really. It shook me up,' she admitted.

'Keep personal matters for off-duty, Cherry,' the grey-haired surgeon advised. 'Business and pleasure don't mix when the business is that of saving lives and caring for the sick,' he added, and Cherry accepted the rebuke.

He was right. She ought not to have flared up at Scott, though it wasn't entirely her fault. If the notes had arrived earlier she could have given him her opinion.

Quickly she flicked through them, after agreeing to meet Mr Atkinson in Caldergate late on Friday afternoon. She would drive there and leave her car in the big car-park while he drove her to the party.

Settling down to read notes wasn't easy, even on quiet days, and she was interrupted again, this time by Student Nurse MacDonald. When her little problem was sorted out she made a desperate attempt to do a quick mental précis of the notes before Sister returned.

Pam Lewin was fifty and post-menopausal. Surgery

had been decided upon for prolapse of the vaginal wall. She looked in a poor state, apparently, but Scott had noted that she was much fitter than she appeared. She had marital problems and he felt a rest in hospital would be beneficial for her emotional as well as her physical problem.

She and her rather younger husband had ceased marital relations and this had put such a strain on the marriage that he had walked out on her.

Cherry read later on in the notes that they were together again, but for how long? she wondered.

They had a new set of students on the wards now, Nurse MacDonald being due to finish her stint on Turner ward at the end of the week, and Cherry decided she would get the new first-year, Christine Deacon, to admit Mrs Lewin.

Mrs Lewin proved to be a short, not particularly plump, anaemic-looking lady, hardly strong enough to stand the trauma of an operation, and Cherry's heart sank.

She seemed years older than fifty, her hair being sparse and iron-grey, her skin wrinkled. Her husband, who Cherry judged to be in his early forties, was reluctant to enter a ward full of strange women, so Cherry arranged for him to say goodbye to his wife in the privacy of the interview room, a cubbyhole of a room where doctors could talk to patients in private, or where bereaved relatives could sit and recover.

Mr Lewin was tall, handsome except for a beaked nose, and extremely pleasant, thanking all the nurses in sight for the good care they were taking of his wife. He called Cherry 'Sister' several times, even though her

badge clearly indicated her status, and she did not take
to him.

His wife seemed less than devoted to him, as well, and
Cherry left them to take leave of each other, knowing it
would not be a prolonged leave-taking.

Nurse Deacon was tall, thin and wiry, seemingly full
of nervous energy and eager to cure all their patients.
Cherry hoped her keenness wouldn't diminish in view
of all the mundane chores that came the way of first-
years.

Cherry and Nurse Deacon formally admitted Mrs
Lewin. Cherry was impressed by the young nurse's
obvious concern for the patient. She even went so far as
to stir Mrs Lewin's tea for her! She also dealt competent-
ly with the woman's questions, apparently reluctant to
ask Cherry's help, adroitly side-stepping those questions
she could not answer.

In conversation, one of the first things the tiny Mrs
Lewin mentioned was that she enjoyed standing on her
head! Or had enjoyed it before her symptoms began to
wear her down.

'Yoga,' she said in answer to Cherry's unasked question. Nurse Deacon was too surprised to say anything
and looked slightly comical, with her mouth open and
her prominent eyes almost standing out on stalks.

Mrs Lewin was not the poor, weak creature she at first
seemed, which relieved Cherry's mind. She enjoyed an
active life. Apart from the yoga she used to go rambling,
swimming, and had attended keep-fit classes regularly,
so she was in much better shape than she seemed on
casual acquaintance.

The house surgeon would shortly be making a thorough examination of her and Cherry left her comfortable and still chatting to Nurse Deacon, to whom she had taken a liking. Mrs Lewin would not be confined to bed, unless she felt really unwell.

The remainder of the day passed more quietly, enabling Cherry to get down to some teaching of the learners. Nurse MacDonald was at the beginning of her second-year and really ought to have known more than she did. She wasn't as keen as Nurse Deacon and could not always be relied upon. Sister would be writing her ward report shortly, indeed may already have done so, and Cherry would have liked to know what her senior thought of the student. She hadn't consulted Cherry or asked her opinion, which was usually the custom. The staff nurse or SEN saw more of a learner's general work than the sister and ought to be asked to give an opinion, for the learner's sake.

'Sister—what about Nurse MacDonald?' Cherry decided to broach the subject boldly when Sister returned from second lunch.

Stella Vinton raised a thin, pencilled brow. 'What about her? Do you mean the report?'

'Yes. I was planning to do some teaching, just for half an hour or so. Where do you think her weaknesses lie?'

Sister shrugged. 'She seems competent enough. Nice little girl.'

'She doesn't know as much as she ought to,' Cherry said stubbornly. 'For a second-year she isn't always reliable, and I thought of . . .'

'For heaven's sake!' Sister broke in. 'The girl is only at the beginning of her second year! She's more reliable than that dreadful Grey woman.'

'Jean Grey?' Cherry frowned, aware that she was treading on dangerous ground.

'Yes. Nasty little woman. Always gossiping. Usually about me,' Sister said testily.

Cherry couldn't deny that. 'She was reliable, though. She did all that was asked of her.'

'So she might have but she caused me considerable embarrassment,' Sister went on. 'She and her friend—another pupil. I forget her name. The things they said about Scott and myself! They got it all wrong.'

'Did they?' Cherry said cagily, hope leaping for a moment. Perhaps Jean had been wrong when she said Sister and Scott were once nearly engaged.

'They spread some gossip about Scott—Mr Nicholson, that is—letting me stay at his house,' Sister said bitterly. 'The PNO had me in. Accused me of behaving unprofessionally—"letting the Royal College down", was how she put it!'

'I thought . . .' Cherry began, and Sister's shrewd gaze swivelled around to her.

'Yes. What *did* you think, Staff Nurse?'

Cherry hesitated, wishing she hadn't started the conversation. 'I understood that you and Mr Nicholson were once nearly engaged, but perhaps that was part of the gossip you mentioned.'

'Mr Nicholson and I have an . . . understanding, Nurse Mills. That much isn't idle rumour,' Sister said carefully, and Cherry's heart turned over. 'As for an engagement,' the woman went on, her eyes on Cherry's face, 'we shall have to see. Let's say it is still unofficial, shall we?'

'Yes, of course.' With an effort Cherry forced bright-

ness into her voice. 'I hope I may be the first to congratulate you when the occasion arises,' she added for good
measure, and Sister beamed.

Sister was so pleased that she even gave Cherry a few
hints on what revision she thought Nurse MacDonald
should tackle.

After that conversation, which confirmed that Scott
was serious about Stella Vinton, Cherry did not feel like
doing any work, teaching included, but she made a
determined effort and was encouraging the nurse to ask
questions when Scott appeared.

They were in the interview room. Cherry had decided
she would give Nurse MacDonald the benefit of some
individual tuition rather than take on Nurse Deacon as
well, and had been appalled at how little the second-year
understood about gynae.

'I haven't got any questions, Staff,' Nurse MacDonald
assured Cherry. 'You've covered everything.'

'Isn't there anything you want to go over?' Cherry
asked desperately. She was convinced that most of what
she'd said hadn't gone in. 'What about hysterectomies?
Are you clear about what organs are removed?'

'Yes, thank you, Staff Nurse.'

Faced with such confidence, Cherry could do no more
than smile encouragingly.

'What organs *are* removed, Nurse?' Scott's cool voice
surprised Nurse MacDonald who jumped up, her pretty
face flushed.

Cherry, who was facing the door, was just as surprised. She hadn't seen the door open as all her attention
had been concentrated on the student.

To her horror, Nurse MacDonald appeared not to

understand the question, or else she thought Scott wasn't serious, for she merely smiled at the surgeon.

Cherry closed her eyes in momentary horror while Scott hovered in the doorway, apparently waiting for an answer.

'Well?' he asked gently, and the student went bright red.

Cherry could understand that. Scott had that effect even on her sometimes! 'Answer Mr Nicholson's question, Nurse, then go for your tea,' Cherry encouraged, anxious not to prolong the girl's agony.

'Please sir, the uterus and cervix,' Nurse MacDonald said loudly, adding, 'and the ovaries,' for good measure, perhaps thinking that her first answer was incorrect.

'In total hysterectomy we remove the uterus and cervix, Nurse,' Scott said sternly. 'Why take out the ovaries if there is no need?'

'Nurse was thinking of Wertheim's hysterectomy, sir,' Cherry put in, helping the girl who looked near to tears.

Scott glared at Cherry, which she considered unfair. It was hardly her fault the student was overcome! He held open the door for Nurse MacDonald who gave a shy smile as she passed.

'I do believe she fancies you!' Cherry said lightly, as the door closed.

'I'm a victim of my own charm!' he smiled. She knew he meant it as a joke on himself but it was largely true. He could be charming when he wanted to be. She could not blame the young student for worshipping him.

'Was there anything special you wanted? Sister is in the office, I think,' Cherry went on.

'No, nothing special,' he murmured, settling himself in the chair the student had recently vacated.

Uneasily aware of his charm, Cherry got up and busied herself gathering together the notes she'd brought in. She could feel his eyes on her and wondered how she might escape the confinement of the room, a room far too small for them both.

'I hear you're going to Amy's party,' he threw in casually, and she stared.

'You know more than I do, then!' She didn't know any Amy but presumed it was the party to which Mr Atkinson was taking her.

'Don't fence with me, Cherry!' he snapped, eyes glinting with anger.

'I am not fencing! I don't know anyone called Amy,' she protested. 'Mr Atkinson is taking me to a party tomorrow night—I assume it's being given by Amy.'

'It is. She's a psychiatrist,' he affirmed. 'Been a friend of Donald's for years.'

'That's nice for him, then,' she said brightly, wondering where the conversation was leading. Then she realised.

Her expression became baleful. 'That was an outsize hint not to get in their way, was it?'

He smiled then, and had the grace to look sheepish. 'They would make an ideal couple. I'm trying to point Donald in her direction but he seems blind.'

'Men often are!' Her tone was sharp, she was thinking of the way he was dangling Margot on a string.

'What was that remark supposed to mean?' he enquired, mildly.

Cherry hesitated, unwilling to provoke a quarrel on

the ward. 'This isn't the time or place to discuss it, Scott.
I have to get back to the ward. Two of the nurses should
have gone to tea by now.'

He grunted his agreement. 'Let's argue in style
tomorrow. It's your day off, I believe?'

'It was but now I have to work until lunchtime. I get
two and a half days off next week to make up,' she
explained.

'Then we will leave our . . . discussion until next
week. Take a trip to the seaside perhaps.'

He opened the door and courteously bowed her out of
the room, and an annoyed and perplexed Cherry went
back to the ward, wondering if she could stand another
drive with Scott. The last one had almost ended in a
lay-by, she recalled.

Amy's party wasn't at all what Cherry expected, though
after Scott's remark she ought not to have been surprised.

The party wasn't in a home but an hotel, where the
charming Amy appeared to live permanently. She occupied a luxurious suite which she willingly allowed
Cherry to roam through, Cherry and Donald Atkinson
having arrived before the other guests.

The decor was a soothing blend of pale blue and cream
with touches of bright colour here and there. The sitting-
room curtains, for instance, were a deeper blue flecked
with silver. Instead of armchairs there were huge,
brightly-patterned beanbags strewn casually around.

'Psychiatry must be paying well!' Donald joked with
their hostess as they sipped pre-party drinks.

The ash-blonde Amy wagged a finger at him. 'You

know I have a private income, Donald! Anyway, there
are the books. They provide the jam for the bread and
butter!' With a beringed hand Amy indicated the long,
narrow book-case tucked away in a corner, and Cherry,
a keen reader, got up to look.

She felt at home there, even in such elegant surround-
ings. Amy was charming and had quickly put Cherry at
her ease. She could see what Scott meant about Donald
and Amy being made for each other.

What, she wondered,' was Amy feeling right now,
seeing the man she loved with another woman in tow?
Her kind heart ached for the older woman and she was
debating how she could best slip away, when more
guests began to arrive.

She would fake a headache and leave Donald to escort
Amy. It would be for the best.

'Good evening, Cherry.' Scott's bland tones interrupted her perusal of Amy's books, and she turned,
smile at the ready.

Then it faded. Now she knew how Amy was feeling. The
man she herself loved had another woman in tow.
Hanging on to Scott's arm was Stella Vinton, her hazel
eyes resting on Cherry without warmth.

CHAPTER SEVEN

THE rest of the party was a nightmare for Cherry and she was glad of an excuse to leave early. Intending to fake a headache, she soon found herself with a genuine one. It wasn't her wish to take Donald Atkinson away from the party but he insisted on driving her back to St Monica's.

She bluffed it out for a while, of course. No way did she intend Stella Vinton to see how shocked, how stricken she was. Once the party warmed up and couples began dancing Cherry knew she could slip away virtually unnoticed.

As she said goodbye to her hostess she noticed that Scott and Sister Vinton weren't dancing. Instead, they were deep in conversation with another guest, the hospital administrator, and that gave Cherry some satisfaction. She could not bear to leave the room knowing Scott and Stella were locked in each other's arms.

It was a warm evening but even so Cherry shivered once she was in the night air. Donald dropped a comforting arm about her shoulders and kept it there until they reached his car.

She was glad of his unspoken kindness and consideration and determined that he should return to the party once he'd seen her home.

He refused, assuring her he'd been to a great many of Amy's parties. 'They're all very jolly. And the guests are interesting, particularly those from Amy's own field, but it won't hurt me to have an early night,' he assured her, brushing aside her apologies for dragging him away.

Cherry felt mean at having spoiled his evening, no matter how much he denied it. She was a miserable coward, running like that. Just because Scott was there with another woman! What of it? If he was playing around with Margot's affections that was Margot's problem, not hers.

'Here we are. Safe and sound.' The consultant pulled up in front of the Nurses' Home and smiled across at her. 'Want me to see you in?'

'No. No, thank you, Mr Atkinson,' she said formally, and he sighed.

'I've told you—it's Donald when we're off-duty. You can't call your date Mr Atkinson!' he laughed.

'I'm sorry, Donald. I'm sorry, too, about taking you away from the party. In fact,' her tone became more confident as she realised how she could make amends, 'I shall cry myself to sleep unless you go straight back to that party!'

When he didn't immediately reply, she went on, 'Please, Donald? I don't want your wasted evening on my conscience, so you'd better go back!'

'Ah, well. If you're holding a gun at my head I suppose I'd better do as you suggest,' he laughed. 'But only for half an hour. Most of the guests will be gone by the time I get back, anyway. I know Scott will have gone,' he added, and Cherry tensed, unwilling to ask how he knew.

'Yes, he said he and Stella would only pop in and pop out again,' he went on, as if she'd asked. 'Got better things to do than sit around chatting, I guess!'

If Donald had tried to be cruel he could not have been more successful. The pain in Cherry's heart grew fiercer as she quickly said goodnight and hurried up the steps of the Nurses' Home.

Although still warm, it was drizzling with rain now, and Cherry thought it prophetic. A dismal end to a remarkably dismal evening.

Cherry was awakened the next morning by one of her neighbours hammering on the door. It sounded unnaturally loud in the near-empty building. The trained staff section was rarely full.

She sat up in bed, her headache returning as the knocking continued. 'All right, I'm coming!' she called out, testily. Whoever it was would get a piece of her mind.

The unwelcome caller was Scott Nicholson, and Cherry glared at him. 'I'm tired and I have a headache, Scott. Couldn't it have waited? Or is it an emergency?' she asked, belatedly.

He shook his head, brushing past her despite her intention not to let him in.

'Scott! I'm not dressed for visitors,' she protested. The brightly-coloured kimono was all-concealing and under it she wore a cotton nightie, but even so it was embarrassing for her.

He settled himself in the easy-chair, his face taut with temper. He was casually dressed in jeans and a pale blue tee-shirt and looked anything but a successful consultant surgeon. Cherry might have taken him for a young house doctor.

Waves of love for him washed over her, and she was deliberately offhand because of it. 'You have no right bursting into a nurse's room like this! Say your piece then go. I'm on duty later.'

Pale eyes blazed at her. 'Why did you leave Amy's in such a hurry last night? Couldn't he wait?'

The sheer savagery of the verbal attack caught her off-balance for a moment. 'Couldn't *who* wait?' she spluttered, wondering if Scott had taken leave of his senses.

'Donald, of course. You dragged him away from that party as though you couldn't wait to be alone!' he accused, springing up.

'We . . .' she began, then closed her mouth stubbornly. Why should she explain anything to Scott? Her private life was no concern of his.

She told him so, too, and he seemed nonplussed. 'That's true, of course,' he agreed slowly.

'Of course!' she mimicked. 'What Donald and I did afterwards is nothing to you. What you and Stella Vinton get up to isn't my concern, either,' she added.

'You gave her a dirty look, just the same,' he accused, and Cherry reddened.

'That's because I . . .' She stopped, unwilling to cross swords with him. Her headache was worsening and she had a full afternoon's duty ahead of her, whereas he would have the weekend free.

'Because?' he prompted, nostrils flaring.

Still she hesitated. Then he took a step towards her and she panicked. She had to keep him at arm's length, pretend she cared nothing for him, or she was lost.

'I don't like the way you're playing around!'

That stopped him in his tracks. 'Playing around with whom? Or what?' he asked quietly. Too quietly.

Cherry was reluctant to say more. He should not need a detailed explanation, anyway. 'You and Sister Vinton. And you and Margot,' she muttered, wishing she could disappear into thin air.

'What about me and your cousin?' He sounded genuinely puzzled.

'Margot loves you!' Cherry blurted out, and was amazed to see him flush.

'Margot *what*?' he snapped.

'She loves you. Oh, Scott! Surely you don't need me to tell you that? She's crazy about you. And I thought you felt the same way.' Her voice trailed off at the incredulous expression on his face. Could he be so blind that he couldn't see how Margot cared?

'Did she say so? Actually tell you she loved me?' he queried, looking so anguished that Cherry felt like crying.

'Not exactly,' she admitted. 'But you've only to look at her to see she's in love! And the way you carried on at her party, almost drooling over her, I assumed you felt the same way,' Cherry finished, tartly.

Restlessly, she wandered over to the window, which overlooked the grounds. Down below she could see the statue of one of the founding fathers. Further over was the medical wing, to the right the large canteen. To the left, in the far distance, she could just glimpse the playing-fields. The swimming-pool was on the other side and out of view.

She didn't want to leave the window and return to their conversation, which was getting exactly nowhere, so she stayed where she was, lost in a brown study. Now she'd told Scott of Margot's love for him perhaps he would sort out his tangled affairs, concentrate either on her cousin or on Stella Vinton.

Strong hands caressed her shoulders, and she hated him anew. Twisting away, she turned, her brown eyes full of tears she could not shed.

'Haven't I made myself clear? Margot loves you! She wouldn't be pleased if she could see you now!' she flung at him, almost choking in an effort to keep back the tears.

'I can't think why you are so concerned,' he commented, his hands dropping to his sides.

'Because I . . . I'm fond of Margot. She's the only family I've got, Scott. I don't want to see her hurt.' When he didn't speak, she hurried on, 'Either you're serious about Stella Vinton or you're serious about Margot. You can't have them both!'

'In other words you think I'm dangling two women on a piece of string?'

Three women, she said silently. But he would never know that. 'That's it,' she said aloud. 'I don't care if you bruise Sister's feelings but please don't hurt Margot!' Her eyes widened in silent appeal, willing him to understand.

'There's no other reason?'

'For what? It's plain enough, surely? I'm concerned about Margot, that's all. She's like an elder sister to me,' Cherry pointed out, and Scott gave an odd little laugh.

'Yes, naturally. You want Margot to be happy. Do you think I'll make her happy?'

'Oh yes!' The words were out before she could stop them, and she bit her lip, knowing she'd sounded over-enthusiastic.

'And if I prefer Stella?'

'Then . . . then you have to tell Margot. Let her down lightly. Please don't break her heart,' she finished, mournfully. You've broken mine and I know how much it hurts, she added silently.

A muscle worked at the corner of his jaw. 'I'll have to toss a coin, shan't I?'

Outraged at such flippancy, Cherry was about to wade into the stormy sea again, but then wisely refrained. No good would come of it.

Feeling young and vulnerable, Cherry murmured that she would see him out.

But Scott wasn't finished yet. 'Having stuck your pretty little nose into my private life, am I allowed to stick mine into yours?' he enquired, mildly.

'No!' She was almost at the door when she flung the word at him.

She hadn't realised he was behind her. Now he spun her around, his hands settling about her tiny waist. She could feel the warmth of his hands through the thin kimono, and knew he must feel the tremor that shot through her at his nearness.

'Scott, please let me go,' she begged. Yet her expression belied her words. She didn't want him to let go, ever.

Involuntarily, her lips parted and he did not disappoint her. As his mouth descended on hers, Cherry wound her arms around his neck and pulled him nearer. The kiss was brief yet searing, and when they drew apart, both were trembling.

'I'm sorry, Cherry.'

Hardly had she taken in the brief apology when he was

gone, closing the door quietly behind him. Her lips
burned from contact with his and every nerve was on
edge. She was jumpy, over-stimulated. Not only her
heart but her whole body ached. She yearned for his
touch, for complete fulfilment. No longer could she be
content with a brief kiss, a caress. She wanted so much
more from Scott and knew it could never be.

The rest of the weekend passed quietly. Sister was
off-duty as usual and Cherry was glad to run the ward her
own way. They were so quiet after the busy week that
she found time to talk to all the patients. Sunday was
always a popular afternoon for visiting, too. They didn't
have so many in on a Saturday.

One of those who did come on the Saturday was Mr
Lewin. Cherry wasn't sure the patient would be pleased
to see him. She was going to theatre at the beginning of the next week and Cherry didn't want her to
be upset. Mrs Lewin's conversation was always full
of her husband—usually his faults. Cherry thought
that, deep down, she was probably fond of him, yet
she wondered why she stayed with him if he was so unbearable.

Jack Lewin tapped on the open office door and
breezed in without waiting for an invitation. She rose
courteously but he'd already helped himself to a chair,
and she subsided again. Clearly he was going to conduct
the interview, not her!

'The wife. How is she, Sister?' He leaned forward
confidentially, and Cherry could smell the alcohol on his
breath.

'She's doing very well, Mr Lewin. She's in good

spirits. And I'm Staff Nurse, not Sister,' she added, with a gentle smile.

'Oh! Yes, sorry, er, Staff Nurse.' He appeared taken aback by her directness. 'She is going to be all right, isn't she?' Again he leaned forward and Cherry retreated from the fumes.

'Please don't fret about it, Mr Lewin. If you show your wife that you are worried, it will upset her. She's quite cheerful at the moment.'

'Think the world of her, I do,' he said, so humbly that Cherry felt mean because she disliked him.

'I'm sure you do, Mr Lewin. Perhaps you would like to pop in to see her now?' Cherry invited, keen to get him out of the office.

He seemed reluctant to leave the room, though, and settled back in the chair, smiling at Cherry. Undeniably attractive, with his big dark eyes and black curly hair, he obviously knew it and Cherry wondered how she could get rid of him without appearing rude.

'Has she made any arrangements, Sister?' he asked, his shrewd gaze on Cherry, who floundered.

'What sort of arrangements, Mr Lewin?' She would not remind him again that she wasn't a ward sister.

'Well, a will and suchlike. Burial or cremation. You know, *final* arrangements.'

Cherry could not trust herself to speak for a moment.

'No, I see she hasn't.' He got up, towering over her. 'Got to leave things tidy. I don't suppose she's going to die but it isn't right to put off these distressing chores, is it?'

Realising that whatever she said would be taken down and used against her, Cherry merely smiled, and politely showed him out. 'Your wife is the second bed on the left, Mr Lewin,' she told him, then perched on the edge of the desk, her head whirling.

Presumably Mrs Lewin was worth a bit of money. That could be why he had gone back to her, for compared to her husband, she was an unattractive, wizened-looking woman.

Glad that no one would marry her for her money, Cherry made a pertinent note in the Kardex. She felt Scott would be interested in Mr Lewin. Perhaps he might even interview the man, put him wise to the fact that a repair wasn't the life-or-death operation Mr Lewin apparently thought it was.

They had two new admissions on Monday and that meant they were full again, as they generally were.

Sister Vinton was on early shift, Cherry herself on another late, which she didn't particularly like. A lark rather than an owl, she preferred to start early and have part of the afternoon and evening free.

She had very little social life unless asked out by Donald Atkinson or by Jilly, with whom she'd become firm friends, so she did not complain about being given so many late shifts. It was the work of the Nursing Officer, Miss Hastings, and not Sister Vinton, so Cherry couldn't say she was being victimised.

Sister didn't comment on the previous Friday's party, for which Cherry was grateful. Indeed, as long as they kept off the subject of Scott Nicholson, they got on reasonably well. Whatever her opinion of her Staff Nurse, Stella Vinton kept her own counsel and Cherry had hopes of a better relationship for the future. If Scott chose to marry her, Cherry amended. If he chose Margot instead, Sister's ire would spill over and Cherry would be right in its path!

On Tuesday Mrs Lewin went down for her operation. She appeared cheerful just before the pre-med was given. Her husband's visit hadn't upset her, nor did she ask to see a solicitor about her will or discuss funeral arrangements with any member of staff, so she wasn't brooding about death, thank goodness.

Her only comment about her husband was condemning, as usual. 'I suppose he'll be at the pub every evening, leaving all the housework for when I get back!'

Cherry thought she was correct, but could hardly say so. She had related the tale of Mr Lewin to Sister, who said she would keep an eye on developments, and it was a relieved Cherry who departed on her days off. Junior Staff was on duty to cover for her and Cherry could hardly believe she was free for such a long time, with no need to don her uniform again until late shift on Friday.

She'd finished early, too, being owed time from the previous week, and as she stepped out into the brilliant sunshine on Tuesday afternoon, she spared a thought for those who were confined indoors on such a glorious day.

Not only the patients but the staff as well, particularly poor Scott, who would be busily operating.

She hummed a little tune as she hurried to her room, intent on showering and changing quickly so as not to miss a minute of the afternoon. It was a last-day-of-term feeling.

Jilly, who was an SEN on children's ward, was free the following day and they spent it together, setting out early in Cherry's ancient car. There were four of them—

unexpectedly so. Jilly's boyfriend, Stu Price, was a student nurse in his third year and had begged for a lift down to the coast as he was spending his days off with his parents in Hastings. Cherry agreed but wasn't prepared for another passenger, John Wise, an over-confident student still in his first year.

Jilly sat in the back seat with Stu, while Cherry had John's company to endure all the way to Hastings. That end-of-term feeling soon vanished! John was older than the average student, having worked in various office jobs before deciding to follow his mother into the nursing profession.

Cherry hoped he was a better nurse than he was a conversationalist, for although he talked non-stop, much of it was trivial and boring. Most of it concerned himself, she noted.

Having dropped Stu off, Cherry hoped they might also lose John. She'd assumed he was visiting Stu's parents or that his own lived nearby, but that proved not to be the case. He stuck to them like glue and Cherry hadn't the heart to drop more than slight hints about his unwanted company.

He was thick-skinned and the hints simply bounced off him. Or else he was so confident of his own charm that he couldn't believe people might be glad to see the back of him. Either way, he was there for the day and the girls made the best of it.

Jilly didn't like him and, being a direct sort of girl, she made that clear, so John turned to Cherry who was soft-hearted.

Hastings' beaches were overcrowded but it was peaceful in the old part of the town. Or it would have been if

John hadn't kept up a flow of what he probably thought was witty conversation.

They were able to relax in a restaurant, over a very late lunch of locally-caught fish, and Cherry let her attention wander, John's conversation washing over her.

It was Scott's round-day. Of course his round would have been over hours ago. He would stride briskly into the office with his registrar and the house surgeon, smile warmly into Sister Vinton's big hazel eyes, settle himself beside her as they went through the list of patients, before he . . .

'Cherry!' John's voice broke in and she scowled, not wanting to be brought back to the present.

'You were miles away!' he accused, his dark blue eyes reproachful. 'And you just peppered your fish,' he added, plucking the pepper-pot from Cherry's fingers.

She gazed down at her plate. So she had, plying the pepper-pot as though it was salt! Well, she must eat it. Concentrating on that might keep John's voice out of her consciousness.

She soon relapsed into her day-dreams, her mind following Scott as he went about his round, asking questions, reassuring, examining . . .

'If you aren't going to talk to me, I might as well go back!' John Wise's voice pierced her armour again, but she just smiled, pretending to be engrossed in buttering a piece of freshly-baked roll.

It was left to Jilly to tell him how pleased they would be if he *did* leave. Although he didn't carry out his threat, he was quieter for the rest of the day, and Cherry had forgiven him by the time they rolled up outside St Monica's in the early evening.

It was still light, though the street lights were on, and Cherry decided she would have a stroll around the grounds once she'd got rid of her unwanted passenger.

He was convinced that because Cherry had been very sweet, she was nursing a secret passion for him. He said as much once Jilly had reluctantly left them, promising to wait for Cherry in the lounge. John had asked her to leave as he said he had something private to say to Cherry.

Once Jilly was safely out of sight, he clumsily gathered Cherry in his arms and kissed her. For a moment she didn't struggle. Surprise and shock led her to stand passively within the circle of his arms.

Then she began to struggle, but before her reluctance became apparent, a furious voice demanded to know what she was playing at. Scott Nicholson's voice.

John Wise flinched away at what he recognised as a voice of authority, and a stunned Cherry was left reeling as he hurried away without a word. Her lips hurt where his inexpert kiss had bruised them. Her upper arms hurt, too, where his grip had tightened when she struggled.

A shudder went through her as she pictured his big, hairy hand caressing her, and Scott misconstrued the gesture.

'You may well shake in your shoes! Can't you find enough men? How many do you need?'

Cherry opened her mouth to protest, but Scott was already striding away, leaving her shaken and breathless.

He wasn't going to get away with that! She ran after

him, grateful there was no one else about. She clutched
at his arm, making him stop.

'How dare you throw accusations at me! Vague ones,
at that! I don't understand what you mean so you'd
better explain.' She was coldly furious, and so was he.

They stood in the middle of the ambulance bay glaring
at each other, before he led her, none too gently, to the
comparative privacy of the senior staff car-park, just
across from the ambulance bay.

'I've been hearing about your collection of men-
friends, Staff Nurse,' he said grimly. His fingers hurt her
arm, for he was gripping the part where she'd been
already bruised by John Wise.

'I didn't know I had any men-friends, sir!' she spat.
'Surely you don't consider that you are one?' she went
on, a little more calmly.

'I doubt there would be room on the rota for me,' he
said nastily. 'What about Donald Atkinson? How often
can you spare time to see him, I wonder?' he went on,
half to himself.

Perplexed, Cherry tried to loosen his grip on her but
without success, and they were still struggling when Jilly
Smith hove into view.

'Are you all right, Cherry? You seemed a long time.'
She sounded disapproving, knowing that Scott was a
consultant, and he abruptly let Cherry go.

'Y . . . yes. I'm fine,' she said shakily, avoiding Jilly's
gaze. 'John just wanted to say goodnight,' she added,
and Jilly made a disbelieving sound.

'Staff Nurse and I have a few matters to discuss in
private, Nurse,' Scott said formally, and Jilly stalked off,
leaving Cherry to vent her ire on Scott.

'Do you realise she's the only friend I have here! I
can't imagine what she'll think now!' She was too angry
for tears, and wouldn't waste them on him if she had any.
'You're . . . you're despicable!' she charged, turning to
follow Jilly, who was nearly out of sight.

'Oh, no! You don't get away with it that easily!' he
snarled, catching hold of her hand and leading her
towards his car. 'You and I are going to have a truth
session. You've played me along enough!'

Like a hunted animal mesmerised by the gaze of the
hunter, Cherry allowed him to push her into his car.

As he drove out of the hospital gates, her only coherent thought was that this was the man she'd once
believed she loved. That love was rapidly turning if not
into hate, then into an intense and burning dislike.

Stella Vinton and Cousin Margot were more than
welcome to him.

CHAPTER EIGHT

It was almost dark by the time they reached Scott's house and he busied himself drawing the curtains while Cherry sat numbly by the electric fire.

She felt cold, so cold that she would never be warm again. Her anger had evaporated. What was the use of quarrelling with the man? He wasn't interested in her views. He had his own and would not be swayed from them. If he chose to believe that she and Donald Atkinson were lovers she doubted that any words of hers would change his mind.

'Switch the fire on if you're cold,' he called from the kitchen. 'Soon have some coffee going.'

She did as she was told, then wandered about the big room, touching a cushion here, a vase there. There were no flowers in the vases and she was busily deciding what to put in each when Scott returned, bearing a tray with two cups of coffee and biscuits.

He'd shed his jacket and tie, and his shirt was open at the neck. She turned away, aware once more that she did not belong to the cosy domesticity of the scene. She was an onlooker, no more, and it hurt.

'Your vases need some flowers in them,' she murmured as she perched on the edge of the wing-chair.

'The house lacks a woman's touch, wouldn't you say?'

'Yes, it does.' Her tone was noncommittal and she busied herself stirring the strong coffee.

120

'Soon remedy that,' he said softly, but she would not give him the satisfaction of reacting. If he had brought her here to bait her she would ignore him. He had caused her enough suffering as it was.

'You wanted to discuss Mr Atkinson,' she pointed out as the minutes slipped by without any further comment from him.

'Ah, yes. Mr Atkinson. So I did,' he agreed. 'I thought you liked him. Bit old for you, of course,' he went on, reflectively.

Cherry shrugged, determined that he should not get under her skin. 'I suppose he is,' she acknowledged.

If she had hoped to take the wind out of his sails she failed. 'What about that young Romeo? The one you were wrestling with outside the Nurses' Home?' he demanded.

'I'm glad you realise that I *was* wrestling,' she said evenly, pleased with herself for not rising to the bait. 'Jilly and I spent the day at the seaside. We had an uninvited passenger, that's all.'

'Why was he kissing you? He must have had reason to hope that the day wasn't going to end there!' he charged. 'You must have dangled yourself in front of him!'

'I did nothing of the kind!' she snapped back. 'He's one of those arrogant males who believe every girl fancies them—or leaves a perfectly good job to follow them,' she added bitchily.

It wasn't in her nature to be bitchy but she felt it justified on this occasion. He had driven her to it.

He reddened, his mouth taut with temper, and she was sorry for her remark even though he did deserve it.

'Our relationship began—and ended—in London, Cherry,' he said flatly.

Words trembled on Cherry's lips but she bit them back. His remark was what she'd expected, so why should it upset her so? She knew there could never be anything between them now.

'What about Mrs Lewin's husband?'

'I . . . I beg your pardon?' She couldn't think what he had to do with the conversation.

'It's reached the PNO. Stella is furious. Says it reflects poorly on her ward,' he said, his voice like steel. His pale blue eyes spat cold fire at her, and she almost felt the chips of ice strike her, pierce her heart.

'What exactly has Mr Lewin said?' she asked quietly, staring into the bars of the fire.

'Only the truth, I expect. You'll hear it all on Friday. Have you finished?' He reached across for her coffee cup and their arms brushed accidentally. Hers were bare, for she wore only a sun-dress.

She jumped as though burned by the contact, and Scott gave a nasty laugh.

'I'm *persona non grata* these days, aren't I? Off with the old and on with the new season's fashions!' He stood over her, the cups balanced in one hand.

Without a jacket and tie, his hair tousled, he exuded masculinity and Cherry coloured fiercely. His nearness was unbearable and she sought for harsh words that would drive him away, keep her out of the danger zone.

He put the cups on the hearth, then knelt down by her chair, and Cherry froze. This was far worse! Lean, tanned hands stroked her arms and she could not suppress the excited tingling that went through her.

'Cherry, listen to me,' he murmured, as his hands caressed hers then inched their way up to her elbows. 'We used to be friends once. Can't we be friends again?' he coaxed.

'I don't want to be your friend!' she cried, wondering how he could be so insensitive. How could he be so blind? Didn't he know every nerve in her body was crying out for him? Perhaps he didn't want to know.

He sat back on his heels, recoiling as if she'd slapped him, as indeed she had wanted to.

'You've certainly put *me* in my place!' he commented, his pale eyes boring into hers, as if he couldn't quite believe she meant what she said.

She averted her gaze, unable to bear the hurt in his eyes. She loved him, yet all she seemed able to do was hurt him, punish him because he didn't return that love. It wasn't his fault that her love was unrequited.

She struggled to find words that would pacify him. 'I didn't mean that . . . that I want us to be enemies, Scott. I . . .' Her voice trailed off, for how could she explain without confessing that it was his love she wanted, not only his friendship?

'You were never like this in London, you know. I thought you sweet and unaffected then,' he said slowly.

Her lips parted in protest but he wouldn't let her interrupt.

'Your only interest then was in marriage, in having a cosy little nest of your own,' he went on, and her eyes widened.

'No! I wasn't out to catch a husband!' she protested.

'It seemed that way to me. You have never had a

real home and I believed . . .' He broke off, his lips tightening.

'Yes?' she prompted, but he made a chopping gesture.

'Forget it. Now that you're fooling around, can I make you an offer?'

Cherry was so incensed she couldn't speak, and he lost his temper again. 'I'm asking you to live with me! It's more than you deserve,' he went on, bitingly. 'I'm not sharing you, though. You will have to give Mr Lewin, Donald Atkinson and all the others the brush-off. Tell them all your days are booked! Not to mention the nights,' he added silkily, and Cherry tried to rise, intent on getting away before the situation worsened.

'I've never been so . . . so insulted!' she raged, getting up only to find herself pushed back again.

'Why? Surely you didn't expect me to offer marriage?' He sounded amazed that such a thought should occur to her, and she lashed out wildly, wanting only to hurt him as he'd hurt her. His proposition was intolerable.

Her hand caught him on the side of the face, and she gazed in horror at the mark her fingers had made.

To her relief he did not retaliate, merely touching his sore cheek gingerly. 'For a slender girl you pack quite a punch!'

Distressed at what she'd done, she reached out and gently touched his cheek.

'Oh, Cherry!' he murmured, brokenly, gathering her unprotesting body into his strong arms.

With a sigh of pure relief, Cherry rested her weary head on his shoulder and closed her eyes. This was where she belonged, rightly or wrongly.

Picking her up as if she was no weight at all, Scott

carried her over to the big settee under the window and laid her gently down. Then he knelt by the side of the settee, his thumb caressing her cheek, then outlining the curve of her soft mouth.

She smiled as he did so, her eyes still tightly closed. Heaven could be no better than this. His hands moved, gently easing down the straps of her sun-dress, and she trembled.

His lips brushed hers briefly, then trailed tantalisingly over her shoulders and down to the curve of her small breasts.

'No,' she murmured, wriggling away from his burning kisses, and he chuckled.

'That wasn't a very determined no! Shame on you, my love,' he murmured, and her eyes flicked open.

He had called her his love! Uncertainly her eyes met his but she saw no love there, only desire as his fierce blue gaze swept over her body.

No! She couldn't let him! If she thought for a moment that he loved her it would be different, but she would be no better than a woman of easy virtue if she let him.

'No!' she repeated the word aloud, sitting up and pulling up her straps. She blushed when she saw that his hands rested on her thighs. 'Get away from me! Go back to Stella Vinton!' she cried, tears streaming down her cheeks. They were tears of anger and embarrassment as much as sorrow.

She loved the man and he was treating her like this!

'Let me know when you change your mind again, won't you?' His tone was frigid as he sprang up, pulling her up with him.

His arms tightened about her for an instant, his mouth working. 'I hope you know what you're doing, Cherry! Leading a man on, then turning cold on him isn't very nice. You are liable to earn yourself a reputation for not delivering the goods!'

He strode back to the kitchen, slamming the door behind him, and a distraught Cherry walked shakily out of the house, leaving the front door open.

She was cold, not even having a cardigan with her, but nothing would induce her to stay in his house or to beg him to drive her home. She began to walk towards the nearest phone box. If she was attacked on the way, she would curse Scott Nicholson with her last breath!

Friday morning brought a verbal summons to see Mrs Green, the Principal Nursing Officer, a charmingly vague lady.

There was nothing vague or charming about her when Cherry tapped at her door. Mrs Green wasn't exactly angry, more reproachful.

'You came to us with excellent references, Staff Nurse Mills. I can't imagine how this . . . these unfortunate events came about.' She sounded sad, and Cherry hastened to defend herself.

'If I knew what these events are, I might be able to reassure you,' Cherry pointed out.

'Surely you know something of the rumours that are circulating, Staff Nurse?' Mrs Green looked her surprise.

'I don't listen to rumours, Mrs Green,' Cherry said firmly. 'I understand—from Mr Nicholson—that I am supposed to have had some . . . relationship with Mr

Lewin. He's the husband of one of my patients,' she explained, and Mrs Green nodded.

'I know all that, Staff Nurse. Mr Lewin apparently spent some time in Sister Vinton's office praising you to high heaven! That slim young blonde sister was how he described you!' the PNO said tartly, and Cherry flushed with anger.

'Just because Mr Lewin praises me, it doesn't mean that I'm having an affair with him!' she protested.

'No, of course it does not,' Mrs Green admitted wearily. 'But Mr Lewin gave Sister to understand that you and he were . . . friendly off the ward. At least that was the interpretation Sister Vinton put on it,' she added.

Cherry burst out, 'She would! She must have enjoyed every minute of that conversation!'

'Nurse Mills! I shall pretend that I didn't hear that remark!' Mrs Green settled back in the chair, clearly ruffled, but Cherry wasn't finished yet.

'There's no love lost between Sister and myself,' Cherry went on firmly. 'We have been getting on better lately, I'll admit, but Mr Nicholson is the bone of contention between us.'

'Yes, I gather that you knew Mr Nicholson before. Were you good friends?'

Cherry hesitated. 'Yes, I suppose you could say that. I imagined myself in love with him once,' she admitted reluctantly. 'But now we are just colleagues, no more than that. From what I gathered from Sister herself, she and Mr Nicholson are almost engaged.'

Mrs Green raised her brows in surprise. 'That's something I didn't know! In that case there is no reason for any acrimony between you. Therefore,' she went on, 'there is no reason for Sister Vinton to wish to cause trouble for you.'

'No, I suppose not,' Cherry agreed reluctantly, feeling that Stella Vinton would be only too pleased to cause trouble.

'Therefore,' Mrs Green went on, warming to her subject, 'she had no reason to exaggerate Mr Lewin's comments.'

Cherry had no answer to that, beyond telling Mrs Green that she disliked Mr Lewin and found his over-familiar manner distasteful.

'That may well be, but there is Mr Atkinson—Mr Donald Atkinson—to consider. I understood—from Sister Vinton—that you carry on with him in a most familiar way!' The PNO sounded shocked. 'What you do off-duty is your own concern but we do ask you to be discreet, Staff Nurse.'

'Mr Atkinson and I are friends. We do not "carry on" during working hours. Or outside working hours, come to that,' Cherry added defiantly, but Mrs Green shook her head in disbelief.

'I have been told otherwise, Nurse Mills. Sister Vinton has already spoken to you on the matter. Is that true?'

Cherry had to admit that it was, but when she began to protest anew, the PNO cut her short.

'That will be enough, Staff Nurse! Please, in future, confine yourself to your duties as a staff nurse. Leave Sister to see the visitors for the time being. She is experienced in handling people tactfully.'

Fuming at this implied criticism of her own handling of

visitors, Cherry left, her cheeks burning.

Stella Vinton and Scott between them had made life intolerable for her. Then there was Mr Lewin. She would have a few choice words to say to him when next they met!

She encountered Jilly when she slipped back to the Nurses' Home with her packet of sandwiches. She felt unable to face a meal in the canteen and run the gauntlet of curious eyes.

It was the first time she'd seen Jilly since the episode with John Wise and Scott, and Jilly did not return her smile. Instead, she was about to brush past Cherry, who burst out, 'Not you, too? I hate everybody!' She fled upstairs, not waiting to see if Jilly might speak after all.

She locked the door then flung herself on the divan-bed. She couldn't recall when she had last been so unhappy. Probably it had been when, at her last hospital, she'd learned that Scott Nicholson was leaving. Then the future had looked uncertain, with big black clouds everywhere.

Now those clouds were even bigger and blacker, with no patch of blue sky in sight.

She didn't want to go on duty and as the fateful hour approached, her actions grew slower. She showered and changed into her neat white dress, and brushed her hair so vigorously that it hurt. Her shoes wouldn't lace up at first try, her fingers losing their dexterity, but eventually she was ready and could put it off no longer.

Walking along the corridor, trying to show a confidence she didn't feel, she was nearly on the ward when she bumped into Scott Nicholson, who was talking to one of his colleagues.

Inclining her head politely in their direction, Cherry was about to walk on but Scott called after her.

She turned, eyes frosty. He was alone now, immaculate and handsome in his white coat, hands thrust deep into his pockets. 'Give you a hard time, did she?'

'If you mean Mrs Green, yes she did! Was there anything else, sir?' Cherry asked, her voice and expression chillingly polite.

'I'll see her. Explain that there is nothing between you and Lewin, if you like?' he tentatively offered, and Cherry quivered with indignation.

'That *is* good of you, sir! And how do you know there's nothing between us? I could be as black as I'm painted,' she pointed out.

People passed around them in the busy corridor, talking and laughing, but they might have been alone, neither of them having eyes for anyone else.

'I *do* know, Cherry. If you refused me, it isn't likely you would say yes to that creep Lewin!' Humour glinted in his eyes for a moment, and Cherry almost smiled, then remembered that she had nothing to smile about.

'If you will excuse me, sir, I have to go on duty.' She swept by and turned into her own ward, twin spots of colour in her cheeks. What Cousin Margot saw in the man she could not imagine!

Sister did not comment on the interview, though she must have known about it. She concentrated solely on nursing matters, for which Cherry was grateful.

As she had been away there was a lot for her to catch up with, particularly new patients admitted or due for admittance. She would be in charge over the weekend, as usual.

'We haven't had any admissions, which is just as well,' Sister Vinton told her. 'But there's one due in on Sunday. She ought to come Monday but I agreed she could come in on Sunday—her son will bring her before he goes back to London. She's got fibroids.'

'Is she for myomectomy, Sister?'

Sister nodded. 'She's forty-one but won't entertain the idea of a hysterectomy. Got a young boyfriend,' Sister went on, disapprovingly.

'Good for her!' Cherry said lightly.

'There's no need for flippancy, Staff Nurse!' Sister rebuked her, and Cherry swallowed the protest she longed to make. She was in enough trouble as it was.

'Mrs Lewin is doing extremely well.' Sister glanced up, her eyes hooded, and Cherry smiled.

'I'm delighted to hear that. She isn't the weak old lady she appears to be. I thought her nearer sixty when I first saw her.'

'She told me she got all those wrinkles because she lost weight suddenly after the death of her grandson. She's been married before,' Sister commented.

'Has the revolting Mr Lewin been in to see her?' Cherry decided to bring the matter out into the open but Sister wouldn't be drawn.

'He's been in once, and I expect he'll be here tomorrow. Keep him out of the office if he does come,' she advised. 'There's been enough talk as it is—it reflects badly upon the ward, Nurse,' she added, and Cherry nearly choked.

Fortunately they were interrupted by Student Nurse Deacon, otherwise Cherry might have been in even more trouble than she already was.

The ward was quiet and Cherry had ample time to catch up on the casenotes. Time to talk to the patients, as well.

She started with Mrs Lewin, whose face lit up with recognition. 'It's been a long time, Nurse! I thought you were on holiday?'

Cherry shook her head, then fetched one of the stacking chairs kept for visitors. 'How are you? Your op went off well, then.'

'Did it? I'm so glad. Am I doing well?'

'According to Sister, you are. I expect you're tougher than you look.'

'All that yoga. Does wonders for you, Staff Nurse. No substitute for being young, though,' she went on wistfully, and Cherry knew she was thinking about her husband.

'I expect you've had lots of visitors,' Cherry said carefully, but the patient shook her head.

'Only my husband. He always comes. I think it's the young nurses he comes to look at,' she went on shrewdly, and Cherry flushed, despite her innocence of any involvement with the man.

'I'm sure he wouldn't come all this way just to ogle girls,' Cherry said firmly. 'He could stay at home and gaze out of the window!'

Mrs Lewin brightened. 'So he could! I never thought of that.'

'None of your family visit? Perhaps they live too far away, but you could telephone them,' Cherry suggested, having read in the notes that Mrs Lewin had four grown up children from her previous marriage and had been estranged from them since her remarriage.

'I . . . I suppose I could,' she faltered, looking uncertain.

'Why not? They will want to know how you are,' Cherry pointed out, thinking how nice it would be if the patient and her children could be reunited. Mr Lewin was apparently the reason why they didn't visit her at home but Cherry knew Sister would allow the family to come outside visiting hours so not to clash with the husband's visits.

'There's a portable telephone. Or in a day or two you could use the one just outside the ward.'

'I don't know. I'll dwell on it for a while,' Mrs Lewin hedged, and with that Cherry had to be content.

The other patients were all doing well and should present no problem over the weekend. They had three other patients who had undergone repair operations of various kinds and they were all together in a group with Mrs Lewin.

It wasn't what Cherry would have liked. If patients with similar operations were nearby they tended to discuss operations, exchange symptoms, give a detailed account of their treatment, and this might vary. Some, too, might have minor post-op complications, and the older patients would take longer to heal than the younger ones. These minor differences could set up an anxiety state in the slower healers and Cherry would have preferred that those four patients were widely dispersed.

If she suggested it to Sister Vinton, nothing would be done. The idea must come from Sister herself, or from the patient.

On Saturday Cherry moved Mrs Lewin further down

the ward, to a group which included two women of about
her own age and Mrs Campbell. She had suggested the
move to Mrs Lewin, so that if Sister queried it Cherry
could say that the patient was happy to move. It would
be better for her husband, as well. In that particular
group, there was more privacy as one of the others was
deaf.

They could, in any case, meet in the day-room. Most
of the patients were ambulant and the less they stayed in
bed the better. The day-room was large and airy, with
pictures and vases of flowers everywhere, usually do-
nated by the ladies themselves.

Saturday was a dismal, rainy day, quite cold for early
July, after the previous weeks of heatwave, and Cherry
wasn't sorry to be in the warmth of the ward.

She and Jilly had made up their differences, Jilly
having knocked on her door after duty the night before.
Cherry felt better now. All she needed was for Mr Lewin
to be prevented from visiting!

He arrived, though, but Cherry was talking to Mrs
Richards, another of the repair ladies, and did no more
than nod politely at the man. Let Sister deal with him
during the week, exercise some of that tact Mrs Green
was talking about.

As soon as visiting was over, however, he made a beeline for Cherry, who was sitting in the office with the door
open as usual, in case any visitor wanted to speak to her.

He came in, closing the door behind him, and Cherry
jumped up, telling him curtly that he must leave the door
open. Her brown eyes blazed at him, and he hastened to
obey her, clearly startled.

'That's better. Thank you, Mr Lewin,' Cherry said

crisply. 'If you have any questions that can wait, perhaps
you should see Sister on Monday,' she went on, unsmil-
ingly. She didn't want to be rude but she couldn't forget
that he was partly the cause of that distressing interview
with the PNO.

Taken aback, Mr Lewin hovered by the door, scowling at her. 'You be a bit pleasanter to me, Sister! I know
my rights!'

People who strutted about telling nurses and doctors
that they knew their rights irritated Cherry. Usually they
were singularly unpleasant people, and were always
troublemakers. She had found them mostly dim, as well,
though possessed of a low cunning which made them
dangerous.

Mr Lewin fell into that category, she judged, and
whatever she did or said she would find herself in hot
water.

'I'm sure you know your rights, Mr Lewin,' she said
soothingly. 'No one is trying to take any of your rights
away from you,' she pointed out, with saintly patience.

'No, I should hope not!' he blustered, then sat down.

Cherry sighed inwardly. This was going to be a long
interview.

'How is she?' He jerked his thumb in the direction of
the ward.

'If you mean your wife, she's doing very well. She
might not have to stay in very long. That's if she can have
plenty of rest at home,' Cherry added, doubting that this
was so.

'We've got a daily woman. Well, she comes three
times a week,' Mr Lewin said, surprisingly, and Cherry
smiled.

'In that case she should be home within the next two weeks, though it depends on the surgeon, naturally. He might want her to stay longer.'

'There's no hurry. I'm managing very well,' Mr Lewin said, airily.

'Good. Then Mrs Lewin needn't worry. Was there anything else?' Cherry enquired, pen poised over her notepad. She didn't want him to linger.

He frowned, then leaned forward confidingly. 'I just wanted to say how much I appreciate all the extra attention you're giving me, Sister.'

Taken aback, Cherry could only smile, though she didn't understand what extra attention she'd given the man.

'I was telling that red haired Sister how kind you've been,' he went on, crossing his legs and producing an expensive-looking cigarette case. He offered her a cigarette but she refused, pointing out gently that no smoking was allowed in the office.

'If patients or visitors *must* smoke they have to do so in the day-room, but we can't allow it anywhere else because of the fire risk,' she explained. 'Not to mention the health hazard.'

'Health hazard! I've been smoking since I was a boy! Forty a day hasn't done me any harm!' he shouted, and Cherry flushed.

This time she would do battle with him, no matter what it cost! 'I am not concerned about *your* health, Mr Lewin,' she said icily. 'I have to think about the patients. That is why nurses aren't allowed to smoke in the ward office.'

He grunted, then looked down at the cigarette case, as

if debating whether or not he could get away with flouting the rules.

Believing that he needed his attention diverted, like a naughty toddler, Cherry rose and smiled down at him.

'I'll let you get home now. I believe you have a long journey?'

'Not that long. I'm staying with a pal,' he mumbled, then took out a cigarette, reaching in his pocket for a lighter or match.

This was too much for Cherry, who strode over to the door and stood by it. 'No smoking on the ward, Mr Lewin! If you have any complaints about the rule you must write to the Hospital Administrator,' she said firmly.

Something in her manner must have frightened him because he lumbered up, thrusting the case back into his pocket. The unlit cigarette drooped from the corner of his mouth.

'You'll hear more from me!' he snapped, without removing the limp cigarette. 'I know my rights!'

'I'm sure you do, Mr Lewin,' Cherry said quietly.

'And another thing,' he went on, by now almost out of the office. He removed the cigarette and waved it at her. 'I've got influence at the Town Hall, Miss High-and-Mighty, and you'd better . . .'

'Yes? What ought Staff Nurse to do?' a chilly voice enquired.

Mr Lewin's surprised black eyes met the light ones of Scott Nicholson, and he seemed to lose track of his thoughts.

'I suggest you come back when you're in a better mood, Mr Lewin,' Scott advised. 'Threats to staff are liable to lead to strikes. You wouldn't want to close St Monica's would you?' he asked smoothly, and the bigger man shook his head.

'I'm sure you wouldn't. I'll let you get along now.' Scott stood aside and Mr Lewin brushed past, still holding his unlit cigarette.

Cherry heaved a sigh of relief, her face still red, the adrenalin still pumping through. She was ready to do battle and Scott Nicholson was the only person in sight. She could do without *him* as an adversary!

CHAPTER NINE

Scott treated her to a censorious look. 'I told you to keep that man out of the office,' he said, mildly for him.

'I could hardly throw him out bodily!' Cherry spat, and a faint smile crossed his lean, dark face.

'True. Any tea going?' He eased himself into Sister Vinton's chair and smiled disarmingly.

Cherry's lower lip trembled. The episode with Mr Lewin had shaken her, and being so close to Scott did nothing for her nerves.

He was casually dressed in a light blue roll-neck sweater that matched his eyes, and dark cords, and Cherry fought down the desire that swept over her. Just because he was physically attractive she thought she loved him. What nonsense! It could not possibly be love. There was nothing lovable about Scott Nicholson.

'Tea?' he suggested again, that mocking smile crossing his wide mouth, and Cherry hurried out, murmuring 'yes, of course,' as she did so.

Tea for Mr Nicholson. Yes, naturally he must have his tea. That was all she was good for, fetching and carrying and waiting on him. Good enough to live with, too, for a brief while, for hadn't he suggested that?

A bedmate. No more, no less. Oh, Scott! Why can't you love me? she wailed silently, as she delegated a junior nurse to make tea for the consultant.

Reluctant to go back to the office until Scott had gone,

she walked through to the ward, stopping to smile and chat. Although the bell had gone, one or two visitors still lingered in the day-room, and Cherry hadn't the heart to turn them out. Some of them travelled a fair distance, as St Monica's had a spread-out catchment area. It included a lot of small, widely-flung villages where public transport was sparse.

Mrs Lewin was in her bed. 'Your husband was asking when you would be home,' Cherry announced, hoping it would please Mrs Lewin.

She looked sceptical. 'Was he? I wonder why he was so concerned?'

'I expect he misses you,' Cherry went on carefully, bending her head to smell the carnations on the locker. 'Shall I put these in water for you?'

'Please, Nurse. He's never brought me flowers before,' Mrs Lewin went on, wonderingly.

Cherry did not comment. Probably the bouquet was to salve his conscience!

She found a vase in the ward kitchen and was carefully arranging the flowers when Scott kissed the back of her neck. She knew it was him because no one else would dare.

'Don't do that!' she snapped, whirling round so quickly that she hit him in the chest with the vase.

'Ow! Trying to kill me, Staff Nurse? That's a punishable offence!' he said lightly, but Cherry didn't intend to forgive him.

'Get me fired, then!' she said irritably. 'I haven't time to fool around with you.' She turned back to the vase, rearranging blooms that didn't need attention, just to keep herself occupied.

'What do you do in your spare time these days?' he asked casually, as she swept past him with the flowers. Her cap was askew, she could feel it sliding down over her right ear, and Scott chuckled at her discomfiture.

'That, Mr Nicholson, is none of your business.' She answered his question firmly, but the recalcitrant cap spoiled her dignified exit and she was forced to put the vase on the table while she attended to it.

'Your hair would look lovely if it was long,' he said candidly, but Cherry pretended not to hear.

Nurses had difficulty managing long hair on the wards, and the caps were never very secure, particularly the paper caps worn by staff nurses. It was easier to secure the linen butterfly caps over longer hair, but then there was the problem of all those grips or hairpins. Her hair was better left as it was. Being blonde she had to wash her hair every other day, otherwise it looked dingy, and it was hard to get grips to stay in such fine, silky hair.

Picking up the vase, she was about to return to the ward when someone screamed, and nurse and consultant ran neck and neck to see what the trouble was.

'Quick, Doctor! It's a visitor.' One of the patients pointed to the day-room, and she and Scott hurried in.

An elderly man lay on the floor. They quickly assessed the situation, and Cherry left Scott to begin resuscitation while she called the nursing auxiliary and told her to set the cardiac arrest alarm system in operation. Then she hurried back to see what assistance she could give.

Scott glanced up, his face grey. Then he shook his head as he knelt beside the visitor. The student nurse hurried up with the emergency kit, closely followed by the resus. team, and Cherry was glad to stand back and let them take over. Her duty was to the patients.

The casualty was Mrs Campbell's husband and Cherry went to comfort her, instructing the student to reassure the other patients and get them out of the day-room.

Mrs Campbell sat numbly by the day-room window while they were trying to revive her husband. Cherry put her arms around the woman but doubted if Mrs Campbell realised. For a time she would feel nothing. Cherry doubted that she would go into shock, the sort that became a medical emergency, for she was a strong-willed woman who had brought up eight children and even now gave a home to one of her great-grandchildren. She would survive.

It was hopeless, and Scott shook his head again as Cherry's eyes met his. Gently, she led the distressed woman away, intent on getting her back to bed as soon as possible. She had, after all, undergone major surgery.

'I'll look after her, Nurse.' Mrs Lewin materialised from nowhere and tucked her arm firmly into Mrs Campbell's.

Cherry was glad that the two women shared the same cubicle. Despite the difference in their ages, they had become friends and a friend was what Mrs Campbell needed now, rather than yet another white-coated nurse or doctor.

Scott would check her over once he'd finished, anyway. In the meantime a nice cup of tea would provide instant therapy.

When the ward was quiet again, Cherry began writing up the Kardex. There was nothing pressing to do until patients' suppers. Mrs Lewin was sitting with Mrs Campbell and one of the more ambulant ladies would call if anything was needed. There was a nurse at the nurses' station, anyway, one who had just returned from leave.

Leave. Holiday. Two weeks of peace. That would be wonderful, Cherry mused, sitting back. Her summer leave was almost due. Despite being a newcomer, she had been allowed two weeks in July, having arranged it before she left London.

The problem was where to go. She had no relatives other than Margot and could hardly plant herself on her for such a long time.

She might go for daily drives, or perhaps take a coach trip. There was the coast to visit, or she could pop up to London. She missed the shops, even the under-ground—much more convenient than standing in bus queues or waiting on draughty platforms for country trains that did not always come.

Yes, she *would* go up to London for a day or two. She would certainly call in on Margot. She might even ring her tomorrow. Margot always slept late on Sundays.

Cherry wrinkled her brow in thought. Was there time to pop up tomorrow? She decided not. Even on a Sunday, she didn't care to drive in London, and she was on the middle shift tomorrow, not finishing until five. She shook her head, and flipped over a page of the Kardex.

Mrs Campbell's page. She had already written of the trauma so she decided to leave it until just before she went off-duty. It would . . .

'Busy, Nurse?' Scott Nicholson sauntered in, then

perched on the corner of the desk, smiling down at Cherry, who tentatively returned the smile.

'Why are you on the ward, Scott? Are you at a loose end?'

'Mm. I am, as a matter of fact. I'm taking Stella out for a drink later but until then I'm free.'

'Oh, good.' Nice for you, she thought, begrudging the time he spent with Stella Vinton.

'Tomorrow I'm off to the big city. Thought I would pop in to see Margot. I'm free on Monday so I could make it a long weekend,' he threw in casually, and Cherry tensed, feeling the pain as his words stabbed her.

'How is Margot? I thought I would ring her tomorrow,' Cherry said carefully, averting her eyes as Scott yawned and stretched.

He treated her to his slow, sensuous smile. 'She was fine last time I heard. Been taking things easy.'

'Has she?' Cherry was surprised that the healthy, extrovert Margot should need to take things easy, and said as much.

Scott appeared discomfited. 'I think she has been overworking lately. I told her to rest up a bit.'

Cherry nodded. Naturally he would be concerned for the woman he loved, or supposedly loved. 'I'm on holiday shortly,' she began, half-wishing she hadn't mentioned it. 'I thought I might pop up to see Margot and have a long weekend. We could go shopping together,' she went on, wistfully.

'I'll take you shopping,' he offered, blue eyes mocking her. 'When does your leave start?' He slid off the desk and wandered over to the pictorial calendar on the wall.

'Hm. July 30th is ringed. Is that when you begin?'

Because his back was to her, Cherry allowed herself the luxury of feasting her eyes on him.

'Well?' He turned suddenly, and Cherry blushed.

'No. It's about the 20th. I don't know anything about the 30th,' she murmured, dropping her eyes again.

'The engagement party, I think. Stella said it ought to be high summer,' he said, half to himself, and Cherry's eyes widened with shock.

Engagement party! 'I . . . I didn't know. That it was all settled, I mean,' she babbled. The words she'd written about the patients fluttered and danced before her eyes, and might have been Chinese for all she could understand of them. 'When . . . I mean, Sister Vinton—I didn't know she was getting married. Though she did say . . .' Remembering that she'd been told in confidence, Cherry stopped. Even if Scott was Sister's fiancé, she ought not to reveal that she knew.

'Yes? What did Stella say?' he asked, eyeing her keenly.

'Nothing. Is she . . . When are you getting married?' She might as well have it all at once. If that news didn't break her, nothing would.

'When? Ah, that's the question. Who knows? It all depends upon the bride,' he answered, with an enigmatic smile.

'Yes, of course it does. I must buy her a wedding present. I never realised . . .' Cherry's voice trailed off and she concentrated fiercely on her notes, even though the words still did not make sense. Scott and Stella. Yet he seemed concerned about Margot. He couldn't love them *both*.

When she glanced up again, he was gone, only the faintest whiff of aftershave lingering.

Tears filled her eyes and she wanted to cry herself to sleep. Yet it was barely six o'clock and she still had several hours of duty to endure. Several hours in which she must appear calm and competent, resourceful and sympathetic. For to the patients, the sister or staff nurse represented not only authority but also a caring mother-figure. She brought solace where needed and reassurance that everything was being done to help the patients on the road to recovery. If Staff Nurse Mills had problems she must keep them to herself. Only the patients' needs mattered.

Feeling not the slightest bit like a caring mother-figure, Cherry brushed away the tears and blew her nose. Time enough for self-pity when she was off-duty.

Sunday duty dragged as it usually did. Mr Lewin arrived late and left early, not bothering to call at the office, for which Cherry sent up a prayer of thankfulness.

The patient for myomectomy arrived as the visitors were leaving and Cherry saw her settled into the ward.

Mrs Lewin was perkier and much stronger now and Cherry knew it wouldn't be long before Scott discharged her. Helping Mrs Campbell was good for her, gave her an interest she would not otherwise have. And, she confided, she had telephoned one of her sons. He and his wife would be visiting on Tuesday afternoon—which wasn't an official visiting time. Cherry had already told her that any afternoon would be fine. She knew Mrs Lewin would not want her son and her husband to confront each other.

The problems some patients had! Having only the one relative, apart from some very distant cousins, Cherry was saved a lot of the acrimony that feuding relations caused. She wanted relatives, though. Preferably a husband and three children! She would even welcome a mother-in-law. Not as good as a mother, perhaps, but she would make an effort to get on with her.

Scott had parents. They lived just outside Epsom, in one of those pretty, unspoilt Surrey villages where every other neighbour was a horsey type. The narrow lanes rang with the clip-clop of horses' hoofs and the friendly greetings of the local folk.

Although she did not belong, she had never been made to feel different, an outsider. Diana, Scott's sister, was a dear. It would be nice to have a sister, she thought wistfully.

Donald Atkinson telephoned her just before she went off-duty. 'There's a concert on Wednesday at the Library Theatre. Care to come?'

She hesitated, thinking of Scott. Today he was with Margot, probably staying for the weekend. Scott and Margot.

The thought hurt, unbearably so, and she found herself accepting the older surgeon's invitation. Why not? There was no point in sitting miserably in her room.

Then she remembered. 'Oh, Donald, I can't! I've just remembered. There's a birthday party in the Home on Wednesday and I've been invited. Your Staff Nurse, actually.'

'Do you mean the big, big blonde or the little Jamaican?'

She chuckled. 'The big, big blonde!'

'In that case, I ought to come. If she's on one of my wards I'm entitled to an invitation,' he pointed out.

'Consultants don't go to nurses' parties! You would spoil all our fun!' she scolded, and he took it all in good part.

'Then I shall set a precedent. Staff Nurse Graham, isn't it? I'll beg for an invitation. We can fit in a concert some other time. The best programmes don't start until September, anyway.'

September. Another two months. By then Scott and Stella Vinton would be engaged, perhaps even married.

No! She couldn't bear it. After handing over the ward and making one final check on the patients, she fled. It was unbearable. She would not have believed the pain would be so intense, so physical.

As she passed the senior staff car-park, a car horn hooted and she glanced over without interest. Then her heart began an erratic beating as Scott Nicholson uncoiled his long legs from the big bronze car.

'Just back?' she asked casually, pausing but not crossing over to the car-park. He wouldn't want to do more than tell her about Margot.

'Yes. Couldn't keep away from the delights of St Monica's another minute. The bright lights of London palled for once,' he admitted, cheerfully.

It was a warm, balmy evening and he was jacketless, his favourite checked shirt open at the neck. He wore jeans, too, which made him look absurdly young. He might have been any young houseman coming back after a day out with his girlfriend—except that housemen could not afford big, expensive cars.

He reached inside for his navy windcheater then

locked the car. Cherry hovered uncertainly. He probably didn't intend to keep her. In any case, he would want to get home. She couldn't imagine what had brought him back to St Monica's—a patient, perhaps.

'Here. For you.' He thrust a casually-wrapped package at her and she stared at it, puzzled.

'You left it in Margot's flat.'

'Oh! My party dress. Heavens, that seems ages ago.' She unwrapped one corner of the parcel, seeing the pale green material. Ages ago, in another life, almost, she mused, thinking of all that had happened since.

'Margot? How is she?'

'Bit despondent. Having some man trouble, I believe,' he said casually, before striding away.

Her startled gaze followed his tall figure to the main entrance, and she was still staring even after the glass doors had swung to behind him.

Margot was having man trouble! Surely the man could only be Scott? He must have told Margot about his impending engagement. Poor dear!

Cherry's soft heart cried for her cousin. To fall in love for the first time at thirty-plus, then to have that love denied her. She would go up to comfort Margot.

She slept badly that night, wondering how Scott could treat Margot so casually. But perhaps he hadn't known how Margot felt about him. He had expressed surprise when Cherry told him of her cousin's deep feelings.

That was it. He simply didn't know. He would never willingly hurt anyone, she knew that. Yet he had succeeded in breaking her heart as well as Margot's. On that troubled thought, she slept.

After a slice of toast in the Nurses' Home kitchen she

set off early the next morning, taking the train up to London.

After two changes of tube, she was at Margot's flat. The quiet square drew her as it always did. The plane trees bent gracefully in the breeze, whispering among themselves as they did so, and Cherry felt at peace.

Here, with the roar of London traffic millions of miles away on the other side of the park, she could believe she was alone. Not even a cat or a foraging dog disturbed the serenity of the scene, and Cherry smiled wistfully as she rang the bell alongside Margot's name.

There was no reply although she rang twice, cursing herself for a fool. She should have telephoned, but she had been afraid to do so in case Margot put on a falsely cheerful voice and insisted she was fine. Cherry would then have had no excuse for visiting and Margot would have been left to cry alone.

It was at times like these that a girl needed her family around her, for it was similar to a bereavement. Losing the man one loved, for whatever reason, was heart-breaking, as Cherry herself knew only too well.

Disconsolately, Cherry made her lonely way back to the underground, deciding that she would go up to the West End. Margot might be working today, though Cherry knew she often had Mondays off.

The receptionist in the travel bureau looked surprised that Cherry didn't know. 'Margot is in hospital. Having it all out, I think,' she said artlessly, and Cherry stared.

'Here. She left this for you, Miss Mills. Said if you came in I was to give you this note.'

Almost fearfully, Cherry tore open the envelope,

seeing that the note was scribbled on one of Margot's favourite notelets. It merely said that she'd gone into hospital for a minor operation and that if Cherry wanted, she might visit her.

If Cherry wanted! Margot must know that she would want to visit. Thanking the girl, Cherry hurried out into the crowds of shoppers.

On the way to the hospital Cherry couldn't help wondering why Margot had chosen not to tell her, leaving her to find out in this roundabout way.

Although it was not visiting hours, Cherry was allowed in and found a pale and subdued Margot in a cubicle she shared with two other women.

Aware that the others were listening, Cherry could do no more than ask Margot how she was. Explanations would have to wait for another time.

'Scott said you were overworking and needed a rest, but he didn't say you were ill, Margot.' She placed the grapes she'd brought on the locker, noting that it was already full to overflowing.

'I didn't want any fuss, dear,' Margot said in such a quiet, subdued voice that Cherry became alarmed.

'You must have lots of friends,' Cherry said, knowing it to be true. She indicated the bunches of grapes, the paperbacks, pretty tissues, and a host of other tiny gifts. The cubicle and indeed, the whole ward, was full of flowers and Cherry assumed most of those belonged to Margot. Typical of her to share her pleasures.

'The girls at the travel bureau keep popping in, and Scott came up yesterday.'

'Yes, I know. He did say he might stay overnight but I saw him come back quite early yesterday.'

Margot relaxed against the pillows. 'He's been so kind. Quite like having a brother.'

'Brother?' Cherry echoed, wonderingly. 'I thought . . .'

'What did you think, young Cherry?' Margot asked, with a hint of a smile.

Cherry patted her hand. 'Nothing. He's never seemed all that brotherly to me,' she added, quietly.

Margot gave her a funny look but did not comment.

Cherry stayed for only a few minutes, promising to return in the evening, Margot having lent her a key to her flat.

When she returned that evening, bearing a bottle of a perfume she knew Margot liked, her cousin was not alone.

A big, burly man with slicked back, greasy-looking hair met her surprised gaze. Brown eyes assessed her shrewdly and she wondered where she had seen him before.

'My boss, Howard. You've met Cherry, haven't you?'

Howard half-rose, smiling a greeting. Then turned his attention back to Margot.

Cherry saw with astonishment that their hands were intertwined, and that they were exchanging lover-like glances.

This must be the man Margot loved! The one who was causing the trouble Scott spoke of. Margot did not love Scott after all!

CHAPTER TEN

FEELING she was in the way, Cherry stayed only a few minutes at her cousin's bedside. She came away still puzzled, still wondering whether Margot had fallen for Howard on the rebound, knowing she could not have Scott, or it could be that she had never loved Scott at all, thinking of him as a brother.

Cherry's head was spinning and she had a splitting headache by the time she returned to St Monica's the following morning. She'd spent the night in Margot's flat and had been grateful for the peace and solitude of the lovely old house.

She returned reluctantly. For once she hated the clamour and clatter of the hospital, the chattering voices, the brisk footsteps as nurses went on duty.

Feeling that she wouldn't last out until her holiday, Cherry listlessly wandered on to Turner ward. Sister Vinton met her, all smiles, and Cherry wondered why.

'Lovely afternoon, Staff Nurse. Had a good day off?'

'Yes, thank you, Sister,' Cherry murmured. 'Did anything happen yesterday?' She had to pretend an interest she did not feel, which was unusual for her. Perhaps she was cracking up.

'No, nothing out of the ordinary. I heard about Mrs Campbell's husband. Poor dear,' Sister clucked. 'She's perky enough, though.'

'I'm glad.' Cherry felt the inertia leave her. Here she

was wallowing in self-pity because she'd been crossed in love, while all around her people were dying. She felt mean and selfish.

'Are you all right, Staff? Not got a bug, have you?' Sister seemed concerned, and Cherry reassured her.

'I'm not convinced that you *are* one hundred per cent. Better pop out to see your GP this evening. Junior Staff will cope,' Sister advised, and Cherry nodded her agreement.

She doubted that it was a bug. She didn't think her doctor could give her a prescription to cure her particular ailment!

Scott was operating. There were not many on his list and he popped into the ward once he'd finished.

Wearily, he slumped down into the visitors' chair and automatically Cherry instructed a nurse to bring him tea and biscuits.

'You eat far too many biscuits,' she scolded. 'You'll be getting one of those pot-bellies!'

He glanced up, his eyes shadowed. 'Like Donald? He's overweight for his height.'

'Middle-age spread,' she said lightly, 'you haven't qualified for that yet.'

'Good wine improves with age,' he murmured, and Cherry shot him a puzzled glance.

Blue eyes gazed quizzically back at her. 'Wouldn't you agree?'

'Agree with what?' she asked, startled. Really, he was behaving in a peculiar way. He seemed preoccupied, tense.

'About good wine. It improves with age,' he insisted. 'Or there's the one about many a good tune played on an old fiddle,' he went on, sounding so bitter that Cherry thought it better not to comment.

Scott's cup of tea arrived fortuitously, and Cherry escaped to the ward. If he was feeling the pressure of the day she would have liked to help him, comfort him, but what was the use? Only Stella Vinton could do that.

That reminded her about Margot. She ought to tell Scott she'd visited her, that she knew about Margot's hospitalisation.

He was still there when she got back, dark head bent over the casenotes, and her heart turned over, waves of love overcoming her. How she wished . . .

Shaking her head, she went out again. To be near him was too poignant. He belonged to another.

A cold hand clutched at her heart as she walked briskly to the nurses' station. Suppose he and Stella were getting engaged this week! Perhaps even today. There had to be a reason for the way Sister almost bubbled over. Something was going on.

She wandered along the ward, trying to speak to as many people as possible. Soon it would be suppers, closely followed by visiting-time.

Busily checking on the patients who had gone down to theatre, she wasn't aware of the surgeon until he spoke.

'Can you spare me a minute, Staff Nurse?' he asked, in a tone that brooked no argument, and she followed him back to the office, wondering what point he wanted clarified.

'Sit down, Staff Nurse,' he said formally, and, wondering and apprehensive, Cherry took a seat. Scott himself sprawled in Sister's chair, his hands together as if in prayer.

Cherry waited. She couldn't think of any misdemeanour she had committed but one never knew with Scott. He was a stickler for rules and regulations, believing them to be for the benefit of the patients.

She nibbled her lower lip, thinking back over the afternoon. Considering it was an operation day, everything had run smoothly. In any case, Sister had been there until four-thirty. No, it was three-thirty, she recalled. She'd left early for a hair appointment. She sat up, indignantly. Surely she wasn't to be blamed because the ward sister had left early?

'You're looking very self-righteous,' Scott commented with a ghost of a smile, and Cherry felt foolish.

'You make me feel like a naughty child waiting to be beaten for some petty offence,' she admitted, her lips trembling as she tried not to smile. 'I've been going over my sins of the day!'

'And did you come to any conclusion?'

'Yes. I decided that I haven't done anything terribly wrong so far. I've been a good little Staff Nurse and don't deserve any punishment!' She sat back, pleased because she'd made him smile.

He looked intimidating when he stopped smiling. He had a stern upper lip, she decided, wishing very much that his lips could be a lot nearer to her than they were right now.

'I have decided to punish you,' he said firmly. 'Dinner at a little restaurant I know in London. Not far from Margot's flat, actually.'

Her eyes grew rounder while she digested this information. 'Are we celebrating something?' she asked cautiously, and he raised a brow.

'Should we be celebrating something?'

Cherry reddened, realising that he had misunderstood her remark. 'No, of course not. I wondered why you were inviting me out,' she said candidly, and his pale eyes grew sombre, the blue becoming almost blue-grey with the weight of his thoughts.

'For old times' sake, Cherry. No more than that. I see you are free on Wednesday evening.' He tapped the off-duty list but Cherry shook her head.

'No! I can't. I'm sorry but Donald . . . Mr Atkinson is taking me to a party.'

His face darkened. Then he shrugged. 'So much for old friends! Couldn't you put him off?'

She hesitated. She would prefer to spend the evening with Scott but at the same time she wanted to go to Hedy Graham's birthday party.

'It's a birthday party in the Home. One of the nurses is throwing the party. I was invited, then Mr Atkinson said he'd like to go.'

'Consultants don't go to nurses' parties,' he said, his voice icy, and Cherry suppressed a smile.

He sounded jealous! Not because he wanted to take *her* anywhere, of course, but because he wanted to go to the party. 'If you brought a bottle or some food, Hedy might let you come,' she suggested, tentatively.

'I wouldn't fit in. Nor will Donald Atkinson,' he said frigidly. 'I'll take you to dinner another time.' With that, he walked out, leaving Cherry to lick her wounds.

Then the supper-trolley arrived and she became too busy even to think about the arrogant Scott Nicholson.

Wednesday was Scott's round-day. Sister accompanied him, as usual, her apron crackling as she walked.

Scott ignored Cherry, not even answering her quiet 'good morning, Mr Nicholson'. Rebuffed, she retreated to the nurses' station while Sister briefed the surgeon and his team.

There was little she could add to whatever Sister might tell him. The ward was quiet. She had already added her comments to the Kardex, checked and written notes on the case papers, so she would be better occupied seeing to the patients while the round progressed.

As she had suspected, Mrs Lewin was nearly fit for discharge, Scott promising that his registrar would make a final decision shortly. She gleaned that information from her once the consultant's entourage had passed.

Mrs Lewin wasn't thrilled at the prospect, and Cherry questioned her about the likelihood of convalescence.

'That's what Mr Nicholson asked. I told him I could go to a friend for a few days if he let me out early. Here,' she beckoned Cherry closer. 'It isn't a friend. I'm going to my son's. The one you saw yesterday, Nurse.'

Cherry was thrilled for her. 'But what about your husband? It won't cause friction?'

Mrs Lewin pulled a face. 'I'm getting so that I don't care any more, Staff Nurse. He stays with me only for my money. We keep breaking up, yet he still comes back.'

'Perhaps he can't stay away,' Cherry suggested. 'He probably misses you so much that he has to swallow his pride and return. That must cost him.'

'Money is his god. He wouldn't swallow his pride and beg for another chance without a good reason,' the patient announced, cynically.

Cherry wondered why she put up with a man who so obviously wanted only her money, and something of her thoughts must have shown in her expressive face, for Mrs Lewin leaned closer, her voice hardly above a whisper. 'I love him, Nurse. I expect you think I'm a foolish old woman. Well, I am!' she agreed, brushing aside Cherry's protests. 'I know he's a rotter, but when you love someone you love him despite his faults,' she added, pressing Cherry's hand as though to convince her.

Cherry needed no convincing. The man she loved was far from being the rotter she'd once thought, but he had his faults as everyone did. Each fault only added to his charm as far as Cherry was concerned. 'I do understand, Mrs Lewin,' she assured her, watching Scott's tall figure disappear into the office.

Knowing she ought to hear the debriefing but not wanting the embarrassment of Scott having to offer her his chair, Cherry decided to stay with the patients. That, at least, would please Sister Vinton.

Cherry was late leaving the ward, a new admission, Mrs Douglas, having arrived just before tea. They did try to take in planned admissions between ten and twelve in the morning and between two and three-thirty in the afternoons. This made it easier for everyone, particularly the new patient. She would arrive at a time when most of the morning rush was over, or after lunch and well before tea.

Some people couldn't manage to arrive then, though Mr Douglas had assured Cherry his wife would be there promptly at two.

Mrs Douglas was a large lady, with a large family. Seven, as she proudly informed the admitting nurse. Her prolapse was severe, which was little wonder.

It was nearly five before a dispirited Cherry walked slowly across to the Nurses' Home. She was tired and really did not feel like party-going. To make matters worse it was raining—just a shower with intermittent sunshine but it could well become heavier.

It was ridiculous worrying about the weather, she scolded herself later, as she reluctantly showered and put on her vivid green kimono. The party was in the Home. On the floor below, in fact, so she was unlikely to get wet!

Bed had never seemed so inviting and she was sorely tempted to have an early night. Hedy wouldn't mind if she couldn't go. It was an informal affair starting at about eight but not really getting up steam until after nine-thirty when those on late duty would arrive.

A nap was just what she needed. Her eyelids began to droop at the very thought, and she was between the covers in a matter of seconds, still wearing the kimono.

There was plenty of time. She could still go to the party. But first, to sleep . . .

Cherry had barely closed her tired eyes when she was awoken. Someone was knocking, quietly but insistently, on her door.

She shook her head, groggily. Had she slept for hours? It seemed only minutes. Then she glanced at the clock and saw that it *was* only minutes.

Angry at being disturbed, she flung back the covers and stalked barefoot to the door.

Her scowling glance met that of Scott Nicholson. His eyes appraised her attire, then he nodded with satisfaction. 'Very sexy, Staff Nurse. And just who were you expecting?'

Gently he put her to one side, his hands resting on her waist for only seconds, but it was long enough to set every nerve on edge.

'I'm not expecting anyone!' she snapped, hugging herself defensively. 'I was lying down, if you must know.'

He frowned, handsome black brows drawing together. 'What about the party?'

'Oh, that,' she said, dispiritedly. 'It's not for hours yet. It won't warm up until nine-thirty anyway. Are you going?'

She glanced curiously at his smart clothing. He wasn't dressed for a party. At least, not an informal nurses'-type party. He was wearing what must be his best suit, of charcoal grey, with a white shirt and a silk tie secured by a gold pin.

He oozed masculinity, and Cherry took a step backwards. Wherever he was going it was no concern of hers.

'I'm not going to the party. I'm having dinner with an old friend,' he explained, looking around for somewhere to sit.

Instead of choosing the only easy-chair, he settled himself on a huge beanbag she'd brought from her previous hospital.

'I remember this,' he said, patting the scarlet beanbag, and Cherry's heart contracted.

'I've had it a long time,' she acknowledged. 'Was there something else?'

He looked surprised. Then rose and shrugged off his jacket, placing it carefully across the back of the chair which belonged to the desk in the opposite corner of the room.

Cherry's mouth opened, but no words came. Weakly, she closed it again. Scott was a law unto himself. When he wanted her to know why he'd come, he would tell her, but only when it suited him!

He resumed his seat on the beanbag, then folded his arms. 'Well? Aren't you going to get ready?' he demanded.

'Ready for what? It's too early for the party,' she pointed out.

'You are not going to the party. You're coming to dinner with me. I've booked a table.'

Stunned, she sank on to the bed. 'Donald will be waiting. We're going to the party together,' she explained patiently, but her heart started thudding at the prospect. Dinner with Scott would be bittersweet yet she could add it to her memories of him.

'I've appropriated you for the evening,' he said blandly, and Cherry bowed her head in apparent defeat.

But she couldn't keep the laughter from bubbling up, and an impish smile crossed her pretty mouth. 'I've never been kidnapped before!' she chortled, and Scott almost smiled, but not quite.

Indeed, there was a sadness in his eyes that was out of character. Though never a jovial, back-slapping type of man, he always had a ready smile. This sad Scott Nicholson was a man she didn't know and she wasn't sure how to cope with him.

'I can hardly get ready while you're in the room,' she said, her mind half on what she was going to wear.

'I'm not going downstairs to run the gauntlet of female eyes,' he said adamantly. 'You might slip away, anyhow. I'll turn my back.' With that, he eased himself around on the beanbag, so that he was facing the dingy wall.

She began to protest but her words fell on deaf ears. Fuming at being ignored, Cherry sat on the bed for ten minutes. She timed herself, wondering how long it would be before Scott's patience gave out.

Beyond moving a little on the beanbag, Scott remained where he was, and an annoyed Cherry decided to accept his unspoken word that he wouldn't peek.

Warily she removed the kimono after she had gathered together all the clothes she intended wearing. Then, as quickly as she could, she dressed. She decided against wearing the green dress she'd worn for Margot's party. Dinner in the West End called for something more formal—at least she assumed they were going to the West End, as Scott had promised her once before.

She chose a softly clinging suit of lilac. With it she wore her cream silk blouse, indeed her only silk blouse. High-heeled black shoes completed the ensemble.

It was chillier than of late and she was debating about the merits of taking along a jacket when Scott whistled admiringly.

Face flushed, Cherry turned on him. She hadn't yet put on her shoes and she felt at a disadvantage. 'I thought you weren't going to peek!'

'I wouldn't peek at you, Cherry,' he said innocently, but that tantalising smile she knew so well threatened to break out at any minute, and Cherry forgave him.

She decided to take her black velvet jacket after all, and they hurried downstairs, Scott's hand on her elbow urging her along. As it was they met several nurses before they could escape into the evening, and Cherry knew only too well what they must be thinking.

'You will ruin my reputation, Scott!' she protested mildly, as she slid into the passenger seat of his car.

'Running around with a man twice your age is worse, surely?'

When she didn't comment, he repeated the remark, and Cherry's lip trembled. If he'd taken her out just to tell her what he thought of Donald Atkinson, he could jolly well take her back!

'I happen to like Donald Atkinson. As you said, good wine improves with age,' she said serenely, and his lips tightened.

Traffic was heavy as they neared London, and Cherry tried not to disturb his concentration. She wanted to ask if he'd told Donald she was going elsewhere. It would be terribly embarrassing for a senior consultant to find he had been stood up. Unkind, too. She liked Donald. He made no demands and had much to offer.

At least he wasn't prone to sulky moods like Scott. If he kept up this silly vendetta she would tell him so, praise Donald Atkinson until Scott was sick of hearing his name. That would put the arrogant Scott Nicholson in his place.

The restaurant was one she'd never been to before. Small and intimate, with tables set a reasonable distance apart so that those at the next table did not give the impression of eavesdropping.

She refused a pre-dinner drink in the small bar, preferring to go straight to the table which Scott had already booked. It crossed her mind that maybe he had booked it for himself and Sister Vinton, Cherry being a poor substitute for his ladylove. Then she dismissed the idea as unworthy of Scott.

They began with melon, a favourite dish of hers. Beyond asking her preferences, Scott said nothing, and the meal progressed in silence. Even the excellent wine didn't loosen his tongue.

Half-way through the main course, chicken in wine, Cherry could stand the brooding silence no longer. 'When I'm taken out for a meal I expect a little conversation to go with the food,' she said tartly.

His head jerked up, his eyes unfathomable. 'Sorry. What shall we discuss? There's the world oil crisis, the political situation, the rising crime rate.' He paused but Cherry did not trust herself to speak.

'Let's see. What else is there? Aha! The cost of living. That's always a good conversation piece. What about nurses' pay? You could make some salty comments on that, I'm sure!'

'Very salty,' Cherry admitted. 'If you are going to be facetious, perhaps we ought not to talk to each other.'

'What does Donald talk about? Weighty, learned subjects, I suppose,' he said morosely.

As he had answered his own question, Cherry chose to ignore it. With a hand that trembled she picked up her wine glass and drank far more than she had intended.

He watched with interest as she almost drained the glass, then the ever-attentive waiter refilled it for her and she took another sip.

'Drinking because you're bored, Cherry?'

She nodded emphatically. 'Very, very bored! I don't know when I've enjoyed an evening less!' she hissed.

Grim-faced, Scott ordered coffee, Cherry having refused a pudding. Then he reached across the table for her slim, ringless hand.

Gently, his thumb caressed her ring-finger and she could not control the tremor caused by his touch.

'I'm sorry we can never be more than friends, Cherry,' he said softly, abruptly letting her hand drop as the waiter hovered with the coffee.

We can never be more than friends. There it is in black and white, Cherry, she told herself as they emerged into the dark night. Only friends. Scott was going to marry Stella Vinton. Margot was in love with her boss—her *married* boss, Cherry now recalled. Where did that leave Cherry herself? All alone with only a career to comfort her.

Even if she had married she'd always intended to pursue her career, though not at the expense of raising a family. *That* took priority. She would have returned to nursing part-time once the children started school.

A sad smile touched her lips. The children, two boys and a girl. Once, long ago, when she and Scott had seemed destined to marry, she'd chosen their names— Scott Junior, John (after her father), and Shelley, who was her best friend at school.

Dream children, waiting on a distant shore for someone to breathe life into them.

Tears burned her eyes and hastily she fished for her hankie. She was wallowing in self-pity again. Stop it! she told herself, fiercely. You're young, healthy, have no physical defects. And one day you might fall in love again.

'Deep in thought, Cherry?' Scott broke the silence, but not until they were back on the road to St Monica's.

'Yes. Deep in troubled thought,' she replied, wondering what he would say if he knew she'd already named the children they would have between them! Would have had, she corrected herself.

'It's after eleven. Shall I take you back to the hospital or do you want a coffee at my place first?'

'No!' she said vehemently. 'I want to go home, please.' Why torture herself and wander through Scott's house, relax in his delightful sitting-room, help him wash up in the kitchen? It was his home and she could never become part of it.

He brought the car to a halt just before the car-park and Cherry was pleased they could say goodnight in privacy.

Carefully she undid the seat belt, wondering if Scott wanted to tell her anything, wondering if he would say goodbye rather than goodnight.

The atmosphere inside the car was tense as Cherry leaned towards the driver's side to pick up her velvet jacket from the back. Laying the jacket across one arm, she picked up her small clutch bag and wished Scott a quiet 'goodnight'.

'Cherry!' The agonised cry broke from him, and Cherry swung her astonished gaze to his.

He caught her up in his arms and held her tightly against his chest. Through his open jacket she could hear the thudding of his heart. Her own heart was beating away frantically as she surrendered to the ardour of his kiss.

They broke apart after what seemed hours but could only have been seconds. Still he did not release her, and thankfully she rested her weary head on his shoulder. This was heaven, or rather a mixture of heaven and hell as it always was in his arms.

He loved another. Only Stella Vinton had a right to his kisses. She mustn't stay. She placed trembling hands on his chest, and he let her go reluctantly.

'Cherry, my dear,' he murmured, but she refused to listen. She wanted no sweet words unless they were genuinely meant.

She scrambled out of the car and ran towards the Home as if all the Furies were chasing her. Tears she could no longer hold back streamed down her face. All she wanted was the sanctuary of her room.

CHAPTER ELEVEN

CHERRY, for once, had a whole weekend off to look forward to, and it didn't seem to matter that she would have to work a split duty on the Friday. Sister wanted the evening off because she was going to the Majestic again. Cherry wondered whether she ought to congratulate her but, as yet, there was no ring in view.

Donald Atkinson wasn't as angry with her as she'd supposed. When she rang him on Thursday to apologise, he was charming, assuring her that he understood about Scott having prior claim.

'But he hasn't!' she protested. She could not break a confidence and mention the impending engagement so her protests were necessarily muted.

He did not ask her for another date and she was miserably conscious of having let him down. She liked and admired Donald. It wasn't fair to push him to one side just because someone more interesting turned up.

She hadn't had a lot of choice in the matter. When Scott had just sat there on the beanbag and waited, there was nothing Cherry could have done to move him. She had been obliged to go out with him, obliged to break her date with Donald. But no more. She vowed she wouldn't hurt the poor man again. Though perhaps Donald would spend more time with Amy now.

Saturday morning saw her in London, heading for Margot's flat. This time she had telephoned beforehand

and learned that Margot was out of hospital and would
be delighted to see her.

Margot hadn't suggested that Cherry stay at the flat so
it would be only a brief visit.

London was packed with tourists, and Cherry was
glad to escape from the hot, sticky crowds. Margot was
waiting as Cherry trudged up the two flights of stairs, and
Cherry frowned when she saw her usually glamorous
cousin. Could this pale, unhappy creature really be
Margot? Her long, golden-brown hair was tied back in
an untidy ponytail, her face and nails were bare of
make-up.

'Climbing all those stairs can't be good for you,'
Cherry commented, thankfully flopping down on the big
settee.

'Howard carried me up. Said I wasn't to overtax my
strength, that he would see to everything.'

'Nice of him,' Cherry said, noncommittally, wondering about his wife.

'I know you despise me because he's married!' Margot
burst out, covering her face with her hands.

When Cherry went over to comfort her, Margot
pulled away, her face tear-stained. 'It's easy for you.
You've never been in love! You can't know the turmoil it
causes, the heartache when you love a man who belongs
to someone else!'

Taken aback, Cherry could only stand numbly, as the
tirade went on. If only Margot knew! Cherry understood
the heartache only too well. Whatever hell Margot was
going through Cherry had been there before her.

At last Margot was spent, lying back in an easy-chair,
her eyes closed. Cherry crept out to the kitchen to make

tea. Margot, she knew, would prefer a brandy, but Cherry swore by the healing powers of tea, proved time and time again in the ward.

Margot was grateful for the tea, and kept apologising for her outburst. Cherry assured her it was all right.

'It's better to get it off your chest. What hope is there—for you and Howard, I mean?'

Margot shrugged, her big eyes sad. 'He's well and truly married. I doubt that he will ever leave his wife. They've children at school and he takes his duty to them seriously, at least.'

'That's a good sign. You wouldn't think much of him if he ran away from his responsibilities, would you?'

'Wouldn't I? No, I suppose not.' Margot brightened a little. 'You're such a dear, Cherry. I feel better now, truly I do.'

After a lunch which Cherry cooked, she left Margot to rest. There was plenty of food in the flat and Cherry knew Margot's friends were rallying around. Howard would pop in after work and she didn't want to be there when he came. She might have been tempted to tell him what she thought of him for causing her cousin so much unhappiness.

It wasn't her concern, though. Margot was older than her, certainly mature enough to sort out her own problems. Cherry had enough of her own.

Donald must have found out that she had a whole weekend free, for she found a note from him under her door, inviting her out for a drive on the Sunday morning.

She knew she would go. Sunday stretched ahead of her and it would be an interminably long day if she had to spend it alone. She could always ask Jilly, though, then remembered that she was going away with her boy-friend.

Sunday dawned, a grey morning with brief shafts of hazy sunlight. By the time Donald called for her it was raining heavily.

'So much for an English summer,' Donald grumbled as he helped her into his Jaguar.

Cherry placed her damp jacket on the back seat, then settled herself comfortably in the luxurious car. She could get used to such opulence very easily! It reminded her that it was time she had a new car, or at least a more recent model than her ancient Escort. She would have another Escort, she decided. A white one, perhaps.

'No conversation, Cherry?' Donald asked mildly, and she smiled.

'I was thinking I ought to get another car. After the luxury of this one, I shan't want to drive my old car again!'

'Time I changed mine. I like a new one every two years. It's a bit too much car for you to handle, though.'

'Hardly the sort of car for a Staff Nurse,' she said dryly.

He looked surprised. 'True. Hadn't thought of that. Still, you will be a Sister soon, won't you?'

'Not just yet. I could have applied for a Sister's post somewhere but I wanted to widen my experience first,' she hedged, not wanting to admit why she'd come to St Monica's.

'Staying long?' He shot her a keen glance before returning his attention to the road. 'At St Monica's, I mean.'

'About a year, I thought. Then I might go back to

London. Get a promotion that way.'

'Will you stay in gynae? There are more career oppor-
tunities in general surgery, you know. Damn!'

Before Cherry could speak, there was a horrifying
squeal of tyres as the Volkswagen in front skidded on the
wet road, then swerved across it, ending up facing in the
opposite direction. Donald had no chance of avoiding it
and went into the back of the small car, but fortunately
didn't join it in its skid.

'Are you all right, Cherry?'

She nodded, dazed but otherwise fine, then Donald
parked the car on the verge and hurried out to see what
he could do.

Cherry followed more slowly, his doctor's bag
clutched protectively to her.

They weren't far from the hospital, but there proved
to be no casualties, after all. The woman driver of the
Volkswagen hadn't skidded because of the wet, slippery
road, her car was in the process of losing its wheel.

It was something that had happened to Cherry herself
once, on a hot August Saturday when the roads were
full of traffic and she'd been lucky to escape with her
life.

'Are you a doctor? Thank God!' the greying woman
said fervently. 'I thought my last day had come! The car
swerved a bit before and I had difficulty in driving
straight. I thought the steering was going.'

'That's just how I felt when it happened to me,'
Cherry confirmed. 'Though my car moved around the
road a lot before it gave out on me. I didn't notice your
car behaving strangely.'

'We were deep in conversation, Cherry,' Donald

muttered, having assured himself that the driver was all right.

There was no damage to the Jag and very little to the other car. By now a crowd had gathered, many drivers stopping to see if they could assist, and Cherry was glad of something to take her mind off the ordeal.

When they realised that Donald was a doctor and could not be expected to change wheels or tinker about with car engines, two drivers volunteered to help put the Volkswagen to rights so that the woman, Mrs Bennett, could continue her journey to the coast.

Mrs Bennett refused Donald's offer to escort her to St Monica's for a check-over, so he had no choice but to let her continue her journey.

They drove ahead of her for some miles, keeping her just within mirror-view, but everything seemed fine and gradually the powerful car increased the gap.

Soon they had the coast road virtually to themselves.

'Endbourne should be nice this time of day. It's still early,' Donald commented, and Cherry forced a smile to her lips.

She tried to appear enthusiastic but failed by a mile, and Donald looked hurt. 'I like Endbourne. Used to go there as a child. Made sand-castles!' he chuckled.

'It's shingle,' she commented, then heard his sharp intake of breath.

'At low tide you can see the sand, Cherry,' he said patiently.

There was an awkward silence which lasted until they reached the small bay and the few shops which together made up Endbourne. It proved not to be low tide, and Cherry could see nothing of the sand where the infant

Donald had built his sand-castles. All she saw was a tide that was still high and a few feet of oily-looking shingle. The fishing and pleasure boats were tied up safely, and there wasn't a boatman in sight.

A few hardy visitors braved the chilly day in their nylon raincoats and sandals. Even the seagulls looked miserable, their mournful cries echoing Cherry's own distress as they wheeled overhead.

It had stopped raining by the time they emerged from the seafront café, and they strolled for a while. Cherry was glad of her jacket, glad of Donald's hand holding hers companionably.

'Shouldn't be allowed, a July like this,' he grumbled. 'Doesn't do my arthritic knees any good.'

Cherry expressed her sympathy for him. Although sorry that he sometimes suffered the pain of arthritis, she was glad in a sense, if it made him want to cut short the visit to dismal Endbourne. She'd had enough.

All the time they were walking, her thoughts had been of Scott. Scott and Stella Vinton enjoying a day out somewhere. Perhaps even in Scott's new home.

She pictured them sitting cosily by the fire, drinking coffee. Sister would have her shoes off, her feet curled beneath her as she relaxed on the settee. Scott would sit beside her, an arm thrown casually about her shoulders. They would talk and laugh. Then they would kiss . . .

Her mind refused to ponder on what else they might do. It was hurtful enough that they were spending the day together.

Or were they? She conjured up a mental picture of the duty-sheet. Was it Saturday or Sunday Sister was off? She knew Junior Staff was having to cope on her own on one of those days, but she would have the SEN as well.

Perhaps it was Saturday that Sister was off-duty. Today she was working. That made Cherry feel much better and she hurriedly pulled herself out of the grey depression into which she'd sunk.

The rest of the day was more successful. They lunched at one of the little town's quaint olde-worlde hotels, enjoying a juicy steak. They lingered over the meal, reluctant to return to the ordinary world outside.

'I wonder if Scott is having a good time,' Donald commented as they relaxed over coffee.

'Scott?' Cherry's eyes snapped open, for she'd been half-asleep. 'I didn't know he had anything planned?'

The coffee suddenly tasted bitter and she spooned in more brown sugar.

'It's Stella's day off. Thought you knew.'

'Is it? I couldn't remember. She was having one day off and Junior Staff the other. I couldn't remember which day,' Cherry mumbled, stirring her coffee absently.

So Sister was off today. She and Scott were together. She shrugged, unaware she had done so until Donald commented on it.

'I . . . I was lost in thought. Oh, look! The sun's out again.'

Diverted, he drained his coffee, and they made the most of what little sunshine there was, standing by the railings breathing in the clean air.

Donald dropped her outside the Home, refusing to join her for coffee in the kitchen or the staff canteen. He had a paper to prepare for a lecture he was giving later in the week.

With a brief 'goodnight', he was gone, and a sad Cherry wandered upstairs, only to hurry downstairs a few minutes later as she was wanted on the telephone.

She hurried because she thought it was Margot, but it was Scott. And he sounded very, very angry.

'You're back, then! I'll see you in ten minutes!' He replaced the receiver before she could comment.

All sorts of thoughts raced through her mind while she waited. She hovered in the entrance hall, not wanting to take him up to her room. He was easier to handle downstairs!

It was five minutes rather than ten when he arrived, and Cherry was shocked at the naked anger on his lean face.

'Am I to be executed straight away or is there a right of appeal?' she asked, caustically.

That pulled him up and he seemed to fight a sharp battle with himself.

Cherry waited, sitting on the uncomfortably hard chair by the telephone. It rang before Scott could tell her what was on his mind, and Cherry had to convey a message up to one of her colleagues.

He was pacing up and down when she returned. 'Shall we talk outside, Scott? It isn't raining now.'

'Your room would be better,' he suggested, but she shook her head firmly and, shrugging, he ushered her outside.

They stood, as so often before, near the ambulance entrance in the shelter afforded by the covered entry.

'I heard about your accident,' he began, pale eyes boring into hers.

'Accident? Oh, that!' She dismissed it with a smile. Indeed, she had forgotten about it.

'Yes, that! You could have been killed!' he snapped. 'Were you hurt? Martin didn't think so. He tooted,' he added, and Cherry stared.

Then she remembered. A car had passed them sounding its horn when she and Donald were pulling away from the scene of the accident. Donald had told her it was one of the surgical staff hooting to see if they needed help.

In her mind's eye she saw the young surgeon's bright blue car slow while he gestured towards the consultant, and Donald signalling that all was well.

'Cherry! Are you listening to me!'

'Mm. Of course. Martin, I presume, is the surgeon. He saw there had been a slight accident and he mentioned it to you,' she said complacently. 'It all seems perfectly clear to me. Was there anything else you wanted?' He was behaving very strangely. Perhaps too much of Sister Vinton's company was bad for him, she mused sourly.

'Anything else?' he echoed, his voice hoarse. 'You might have been killed!' He emphasised the point by shaking her.

When he let her go, they were both shocked at his vehemence. 'I apologise,' he said stiffly. 'I thought . . . You could have had a nasty accident,' he went on, his voice controlled again.

Cherry made light of it. 'I think your friend Martin has been exaggerating! Some poor woman lost a wheel from her car. Though that is an exaggeration, too!' she said impishly. 'The wheel worked loose and had to be retightened. It could have been nasty. It happened to me once.'

'Did it? When? You didn't tell me!' He towered over her, as though accusing her of some heinous crime.

'It was when I worked in London. I was on my way to Bath to fetch Margot, as a matter of fact. Her car was up the creek and I'd volunteered . . .' Her voice trailed off. Why on earth should she tell him all this?

'Is there anything else, Scott? I have a headache and I want an early night.'

'Do you?' he said softly, and she coloured at the implication.

'I'm on early duty tomorrow. That means getting up at six o'clock,' she pointed out coldly. 'Can I go now or do you want any more information?'

Hands on slim hips, she defied him. Then she deliberately moved closer, knowing the perfume she was wearing was his favourite. Let him have the full treatment! Out of the corner of her eye she saw Sister Vinton approaching and knew Scott wasn't aware of that.

'It's sweet of you to worry about me, Scott,' she smiled, placing a small hand on his arm.

His tortured gaze rested on her for a moment and everyone ceased to exist, even Sister Vinton.

'Cherry—I want . . .' he began, and Cherry held her breath.

Then Sister's honeyed tones broke in on what might have become an interesting conversation, and Scott turned away without another word.

Sister appeared not to recognise Cherry in mufti, and spared her no more than a casual glance. Then she and

Scott strolled away, Sister laughing at some remark of his.

Disconsolately, Cherry watched for a moment. The lovers. And she had been stupid enough to believe she could influence Scott's feelings for her!

Yet he seemed so concerned, so distressed about the accident. That must mean he cared. Perhaps only because she was an old friend.

Whatever the truth of the matter, Scott had gone willingly enough with Stella Vinton, his 'friend' conveniently forgotten.

The week sped by because they were so busy, including an emergency admission. Mrs Lewin was discharged, supposedly to a convalescent home but really to her son's care. What her husband didn't know couldn't grieve him, seemed to be Mrs Lewin's philosophy.

Mrs Campbell wasn't due for discharge yet. She hadn't recovered from the shock of her husband's death and although they needed the bed, Scott kept her in for a while longer than he might otherwise have done.

On Friday morning Sister Vinton appeared, all smiles, and took Cherry aside. Wondering what was coming but fearing the worst, Cherry waited.

Sister fingered the chain about her neck. Cherry couldn't see what was on the chain but assumed it to be a locket bearing Scott's photograph.

But it wasn't. It was a ring. A small sparkling sapphire with diamond-set shoulders. Dully Cherry watched as Sister slipped it on, flexing her fingers so that it flashed when the light caught it.

'It's magnificent, Sister,' Cherry breathed, aware of

the woman's sharp gaze. Truly it was. Though small, the stone threw out so much blue fire that Cherry was dazzled.

'It *is* nice, isn't it,' Sister agreed, slipping the ring back on to the chain again. 'Pity I can't wear it on duty. Have to keep it hidden away!' she chuckled.

Although crying inwardly, Cherry offered Sister her congratulations. It was Sister's good fortune and Cherry's hard luck. There was no more to be said.

Deciding to put Scott right out of her mind, Cherry made out a list of activities and goals designed to do just that. By the end of her year at St Monica's Cherry Mills would be a new woman!

First on the list was a new hair-style. Because her hair was short and fine there was a limit to what could be done. Nevertheless, on her next day off Cherry treated herself to a new style, softer and fuller on the top, with tendrils just curving round the front of her ears.

She bought loads of new make-up and experimented with it even when she was tired after a long day. A professional make-up lesson was an investment, she decided, and made an appointment with a London salon.

New clothes would have been nice but that was an extravagance she resisted to some extent.

In the end the only clothes she bought were two pairs of smart court shoes and a new pair of sandals for the holidays, plus a bikini with a matching top and skirt.

She wasn't too sure about the bikini. It looked well enough when she wore it in the privacy of her room but she lacked the courage to try it out when using the staff swimming-pool! She would wear it at Endbourne on her holiday.

She thought about a new party dress, but she wasn't a party person. The money she had intended to pay out for a new dress she sent instead to a local charity. Their need was greater than hers.

That just left a replacement for her old car. Money spent on a newer car wasn't money wasted. If she looked after it carefully it would last for years. It would have to!

Jilly's boyfriend knew a lot about cars and the three of them spent happy hours peering at second-hand cars or following up adverts in the paper, but without success. Those Cherry liked proved to be either too expensive or not worth the money asked. A lot suffered from rust and Cherry wondered why more owners didn't have their cars rust-proofed.

Deciding that she would have to order a new one and ask for hire-purchase, Cherry was peering in a car showroom in Caldergate when Donald called to her.

She hadn't seen him since the unfortunate day at Endbourne, but he greeted her cheerfully enough.

'Why don't you get a car that's two or three years old? They've got over most of their teething problems by then,' he told her.

In the end he helped her to find a vivid red car less than a year old. One of his private patients was selling it. 'He bought it for his fancy-woman but she left him before he could give it to her!' Donald laughed.

Longingly, Cherry ran her hand over the little car's smooth paintwork. She must have it! Why, it looked like new. Loath though she was to part with her old one, she wanted a change. A newish car would make her feel a new woman. It was all change for Cherry Mills!

Cherry found herself in demand with the male members of the staff. With her new hair-do and her new image she became popular beyond her wildest expectations. John Wise hung around her, his fear of Scott forgotten, and she took the greatest pleasure in telling him exactly what she thought of him, and he beat a hasty retreat.

When she went up to see a fully-recovered Margot, even her cousin was taken aback.

'I'm thrilled for you, Cherry! You're almost beautiful. Not quite, but almost!' Margot said candidly.

Cherry didn't believe her. She only wished her new-style self could find some new-style happiness, but it wasn't to be.

On-duty, of course, she appeared no different, with her hair pushed out of its style by the paper cap. She wore little make-up on duty.

Scott might have been a complete stranger for all the notice he took of her. He and Sister spent much time deep in conversation, which was only to be expected with the engagement party only a matter of days away.

Cherry, thankfully, would miss it—not that Sister had invited her, anyway. Her holiday was almost due and she could forget the ward, forget Scott, for two whole weeks.

The vivid red car attracted attention and received many admiring glances, usually from female staff. The men, she found, were interested only in its price and how many miles it did to the gallon!

Scott apparently didn't know about the car until the

morning of her holiday. It was a gloriously sunny day, the rain of the past weeks seeming no more than a dream.

Cherry had intended trying out her new bikini at Endbourne. Then she saw that the hospital pool was almost empty at this early hour. Only a couple of female students splashed about in the shallow end.

Seizing the opportunity for a private swim and a chance to christen her bikini, she stripped off her blue and gold dress revealing the clinging silver-grey bikini underneath.

She climbed the board, intent on diving in. There was a wonderful holiday atmosphere around—though it may have emanated from Cherry herself who had two weeks of freedom. Two weeks away from Scott's uncaring gaze.

As she dived, visions of Scott floated on the water below. Her body cleaved the water, causing ripples in which she could still see his face, his pale, heavy-lidded eyes, that sexy mouth . . .

She swam for a few minutes, watched admiringly by the young nurses, then clambered out, the bikini clinging provocatively to her figure.

She enveloped herself in her beach-towel then sensed that she was being watched.

A sombre-faced Scott Nicholson leaned against the wall of the changing-hut, his eyes on her.

It was as she'd imagined. His eyes were half-closed, the dark lashes long and curling against his cheeks. The sexy smile was absent, though, and Cherry deliberately ignored him, intent on going to the hut to change before her day at the seaside.

He gave no sign that he'd seen her. He was dressed for a day out, in jeans and a bright green tee-shirt.

Thinking how absurdly young he looked, Cherry hurriedly dried then rolled up the wet bikini. She probably wouldn't want to bathe at Endbourne now but would find a quiet part of the beach simply to sit and stare.

'I see you have another car,' Scott said, the moment she emerged. He'd moved and was only inches from her as she hovered in the doorway of the hut.

'Yes, isn't it lovely! Time I had a change.'

'It isn't new. I should have thought he could have run to a newer model,' he went on tightly, and Cherry stared, not understanding.

'The owner *has* a newer model, I expect. But this was a second car and he found he didn't need it any more,' she explained.

'You mean it belonged to Donald?'

She shook her head, spray from her damp hair sprinkling his tee-shirt. She wished she'd worn a cap, wanting him to see her new hair-style at its best. Not that he would care, of course.

'Shouldn't you be escorting Sister Vinton?' she enquired sweetly. 'She wouldn't be very pleased if she could see you hanging around the ladies' changing-hut,' she couldn't resist adding, but the barb didn't penetrate his tough skin.

'You didn't answer my question! Did that car belong to Donald Atkinson?' His face was working as he fought to hold back his temper.

'No, the car did not belong to Donald. It belonged to a patient of his, actually,' she admitted, and immediately he seized on that.

'Ah! Then he bought it from the patient and gave it to you!'

When, shocked, she didn't answer, he went on, 'Did he, Cherry? Answer me! Did Atkinson buy you that car?'

Wonderingly, she shook her head. If she didn't know better she would believe him jealous!

'Are you sure?' He appeared not to believe her, but if he chose not to, there was nothing she could do about it.

Summoning up a smile she managed to offer him her congratulations upon his engagement. 'I know it isn't official yet, you said the party wasn't until next week, but Sister showed me her ring recently and . . . and I want you to know that I wish you all the happiness in the world.' Her voice faltered towards the end, but he wouldn't notice.

All that nonsense about Donald Atkinson! Scott didn't care one way or the other. He wanted his own pleasures but didn't want her to have any fun!

Indignantly, she turned back to tell him what she thought of him, but their bodies collided, and she found herself in much closer contact with him than she had expected.

His breath warmed her face, the aroma of his aftershave tantalized her nostrils. His nearness almost overcame her resolution to put him from her mind forever.

'Stella is engaged but I'm not,' he said softly. His eyes were on her, as if begging her to understand.

Which she did not. 'I thought that you and she . . . I mean, she *said* you were going to make an announcement,' she protested.

He shook his head, then trailed a finger down the side

of her face. 'No, no. She did think at one time that we were getting engaged,' he admitted. 'Though where she got that idea from is beyond me! It was before you came, anyway.'

'Who . . . who is she marrying?' She could hardly get the words out, the mounting excitement within causing her to lose track of her thoughts. Scott wasn't engaged. He was free!

'The Administrator, would you believe!'

'They kept it very quiet. I thought she was marrying you!'

'He's divorced. I think he wanted to be sure this time. Stella and I remained friends, and if the grapevine got the wrong impression, well, neither of us did anything to correct it. It meant Stella and Chris could keep their romance a secret and it didn't harm me.'

There was an awkward pause, and Cherry smiled without actually meeting his intent gaze. He was fancy-free but that did not mean he loved or even wanted Cherry Mills.

Of course he had once asked her to live with him. She wondered if that offer was still going. It wasn't what she wanted, but . . .

She licked her dry lips, not knowing where to begin, not knowing if she had the cheek to throw herself at him. Supposing he no longer wanted her?

If he did and she went to him on his terms, wouldn't it be possible for him to love her one day?

She opened her mouth to speak the fateful words, knowing that if he rebuffed her she would leave St Monica's.

He leaned towards her again, his eyes almost pleading, wishing the words out of her mouth, almost. 'Yes?' he asked, and she nodded, too full to speak.

Full of gratitude that he'd saved her from actually offering herself, she went willingly into his arms, giving him back kiss for kiss.

Her heart swelled with joy. It wasn't as good as marriage—nothing ever could be—and he didn't love her. Yet he might, one day!

'Oh, Cherry, my darling!' He hugged her even closer and she went dizzy with need of him. 'We can't stay here. Consultants don't frequent the swimming-pool!' he joked, and Cherry remembered that she'd thought the same thing all those weeks ago. Though she had visualised the athletic Scott taking a quiet dip sometimes.

Hand in hand they strolled towards Scott's car.

'Where are we going? I was off to Endbourne,' she said shyly. 'Thought I would give my bikini an airing there!'

'It's a lovely bikini,' he assured her, his gaze melting her resistance. 'But keep it just for me. I don't see why Mr Scott Nicholson's wife should provide the people of Endbourne with a free show!'

When she hung back, he turned puzzled eyes on her. 'You aren't having second thoughts, are you, love? I thought . . .'

'Yes?'

'I thought we could go into Tunbridge Wells. Or London, if you prefer. Get the engagement ring today—before you change your mind. Cherry, say something!'

Eyes shining, Cherry stood on tiptoe and kissed him in full view of a couple of ambulance men who were about to drive off.

He reddened, and Cherry chuckled. 'Sorry, Mr Nicholson!'

The ambulance men grinned and waved to them as they drove off.

'You *will* marry me, won't you?'

'Yes, Mr Nicholson,' she said pertly, her heart filled with love for him. 'When you asked—I mean, I thought you meant just to live with you,' she admitted.

'And you would have done?' he demanded.

'You did ask me once . . .' she began, but he broke in.

'That was because . . . I thought you were playing the field. I didn't really mean it. I've always loved you, Cherry. You were always my choice, but when we were in London I wanted to concentrate on my career, on becoming a good surgeon. Knowing how keen you were on setting up home, I didn't dare get too involved. I didn't think I could be a good husband *and* a good surgeon. My work had to come before my personal happiness.'

She nodded, understandingly. 'That was why you came to St Monica's?'

'Partly,' he agreed. 'I had to move to a smaller hospital for my first consultant's post. I need not have moved quite so soon, I could have waited, married you there, but I needed to find my feet. Do you understand, Cherry?'

'Of course. Do *you* understand that I love you very much?'

His kiss told her that he did.

Doctor Nurse Romances

Romance in modern medical life

Read more about the lives and loves of doctors and nurses in the fascinatingly different backgrounds of contemporary medicine. These are the four Doctor Nurse romances to look out for next month.

A NAVAL ENGAGEMENT
Elspeth O'Brien

MATCHMAKER NURSE
Betty Beaty

STAFF NURSE ON GLANELLY WARD
Janet Ferguson

DR PILGRIM'S PROGRESS
Anne Vinton

Buy them from your usual paperback stockist, or write to: Mills & Boon Reader Service, P.O. Box 236, Thornton Rd, Croydon, Surrey CR9 3RU, England. Readers in South Africa-write to: Mills & Boon Reader Service of Southern Africa, Private Bag X3010, Randburg, 2125.

Mills & Boon
the rose of romance

Doctor Nurse Romances

Amongst the intense emotional pressures of modern medical life, doctors and nurses often find romance. Read about their lives and loves in the other three Doctor Nurse titles available this month.

NURSE AT TWIN VALLEYS
by Lilian Darcy

Love on the rebound is definitely not for Nurse Orana Bowe. She has come to work at the Australian ski resort of Twin Valleys to escape from a broken heart, so she is determined not to fall for the first man she meets just because he resembles Dr Jack de Salis . . .

DOCTOR'S DIAGNOSIS
by Grace Read

In her new role as Sister at St Benedict's Gina Brent has more important issues to think about than the outrageously antagonistic behaviour of Dr Russell Steele. But when Dr Steele goes out of his way to be charming can she stop herself from loving him?

THE END OF THE RAINBOW
by Betty Neels

As a grateful niece, Olympia feels bound to work in her aunt's nursing home, though her life is little more than that of a dogsbody. Then fate takes a hand in the form of Dr Waldo van der Graaf . . .

Mills & Boon
the rose of romance

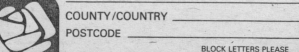